THE AMISH SECRET SANTA

HANNAH SCHROCK

CHAPTER 1

"*K*umm on, Leah, you love apple strudel at Christmas," Hannah Fisher said to her younger sister, who seemed very reluctant to help with the preparations.

Leah looked sad; not sullen, like many teenagers might when asked to help in the kitchen, but genuinely sad.

"I know, it's just…"

Her words trailed off as she turned away from her sister, wiping her face with her arm. It was clear she was rubbing tears from her eyes.

"*Kumm* on, you know *Daed* wouldn't want us to feel this way," Hannah said, pulling the fifteen-year-old into her arms.

Leah buried her head into her sister's shoulder.

Despite being three years younger, Leah was already two inches taller than Hannah.

"It just won't be the same anymore," Leah spluttered.

Hannah swallowed, trying to push down the emotions that filled her own chest. The last few years had been terribly hard on everyone, but especially on Hannah.

Three years ago, their mother died. It was an illness that quickly consumed her. Hannah had noticed her mother getting tired, and then weaker, and within seven weeks, she was gone. Cancer: that's what the *Englisch* doctor had said.

After that, Hannah, who was just fifteen years old at the time, having left school the year before, was forced to take over running the household. She stepped into the role of mother as well as older sister almost without thinking.

Her father battled on, doing his best despite the heart-breaking grief. He worked harder than ever to ensure there was enough money coming in to look after them all and to build a small rainy-day fund for his children. He worked at a factory in town, employed by the *Englisch*.

Their Amish community was relatively progressive, and such practices were not only allowed by the bishop but encouraged. He knew that for the long-term prosperity of the community, not everyone could work on farms or in traditional businesses like carpentry. Jobs with the *Englisch* were simply considered normal.

The problem was that Daniel Fisher was working too hard. He was taking overtime shifts when he shouldn't have, pleased to have the chance to earn more money. Of course, it wasn't just the money that drove him. Working long hours helped him forget the pain of losing his beloved wife.

Six months ago, he was riding home in his buggy, exhausted, when he collapsed at the reins. Other members of the community found him just after dawn the next morning, still sitting in the buggy at the side of a country road. He had been dead for hours.

Heartbreak and overwork had killed him. And now, Hannah was forced to not only be a sister and a mother, but a father as well.

Fortunately, Leah had finished school the previous year and was now able to help with some of the tasks at home. Their father had indeed left them a small nest egg. It would probably be enough to ensure that Hannah didn't need to work until twelve-year-old Aaron finished school in two years.

If she was frugal, she might be able to stretch the funds for another year. She had already taken on some small sewing jobs from the *Englischers* in town to help pay for little treats for her siblings. Leah was still young at fifteen, and Hannah didn't want to confine her to the house at that age. She wanted to give her time to go out with her friends, enjoy a coffee in town, or get a doughnut from the bakery. These little sewing jobs helped pay for that.

It was now seven days until Christmas. The snow started falling the previous day. Usually, that was cause for great excitement in the household. Rachel, who was only seven, still found the wonder in such events. To some extent, young Aaron did too, as it provided a welcome distraction from school which he detested attending.

But for Leah and Hannah, it only brought sadness.

Their parents had both adored the Christmas season. And now, with the first Season approaching since they were both gone, they knew it would be a time of sorrow rather than celebration.

"We need to make the apple strudel. *Daed* used to love it. Do you remember?" Hannah said, trying to be uplifting. "We have to make it for him."

Leah sighed and wiped her eyes, moving over to the kitchen counter.

"*Gut* girl," Hannah said as Leah started getting to work.

"I don't know how you've managed these last few years, Hannah. You've been so strong, so brave."

Hannah smiled and nervously tucked that annoying strand of brown hair that always popped out of her *kapp* back under it. The truth was, she had been anything but brave. Night after night, she would go to bed and cry herself to sleep over the loss of their mother. She knew she could never be a sufficient replacement. All she could do was her best, and that's what she got up each morning to try to do.

She owed it to her mother's memory.

"Don't be silly," Hannah said, a tear coming to her own eye now. She turned to the stove and pulled out the fruitcake she had put there after dropping Leah and Aaron at school that morning. It smelled delicious, filling the air with all the aromas of Christmas.

Despite her positive attitude, she knew Leah was right about it not being the same this year. But it was something she knew they had to get through. After all, the clock wouldn't stop ticking just because they were all grieving.

"Do you want to *kumm* with me to fetch the *kinner* from school?" Hannah asked, sensing that Leah was still struggling with sadness. A walk in the fresh air would do her good. The apple strudel could wait until they returned. Rachel might even decide to help, although she would probably be more of a hindrance, but it would keep her entertained for an hour.

Leah nodded. "I'd like that."

"*Kumm* on, then. We had better wrap up though. It was icy this morning."

Both women washed their hands and pulled on their coats and boots. The snow had been falling gently but steadily throughout the day, accumulating on the ground and turning the fields and hills white. Hannah always loved snowfall at Christmas. It made everything feel more magical in a way. But this year, it just seemed to be yet another hindrance.

They walked swiftly to the schoolhouse, enjoying the crunch of snow under their boots. They chatted aimlessly as they went, carefully avoiding the topic of Christmas as well as the loss of their parents.

The children were just starting to run out of the schoolhouse when they arrived. Other members of the Amish community greeted them, some with warm smiles, others with sad, sympathetic words.

Hannah often wished they would stop. She didn't want to be constantly reminded of the loss.

There were squeals of delight from the children as they ran out, many of them tossing snowballs at each other. Aaron was right in the middle of it all.

Hannah couldn't help but smile at him. His tousled blond hair contrasted with the dark shades of the rest of the family. He had always been the different one. While everyone else was quiet and reserved, he was loud and boisterous, always breaking as many rules as he could.

Hannah had found him a challenge to manage at times. Occasionally, he would come back with, "You're not my *mamm*," which wounded her greatly. But he was just a child being a child. After saying such hurtful words, he would later come and apologize. Despite his wild nature, he was a good boy at heart.

"*Kumm* on, we've got lots of baking to do at home to prepare for the next few days. Let's not mess around," Hannah told Rachel and Aaron as soon as they joined the two older siblings outside of the school.

Aaron, of course, had other ideas as they started their walk back home. He began by throwing a snowball at Rachel, who squealed with delight when it hit her square in the back. She turned and returned fire, though her snowball barely reached Aaron's feet. Then Leah decided to join in, sticking up for her younger sister. Her snowball was bigger, aimed perfectly, and hit Aaron right on the nose.

He returned fire with vengeance, and Hannah watched, a smile creeping onto her face as her three younger siblings played in the snow, almost as if they didn't have a care in the world.

"That almost hit my horse," a gruff voice came from a buggy passing by. "You need to be more careful."

It was Noah Beiler, a strange man who lived on the far edge of the community. He hardly integrated with anyone, living on his own as he did, and most people found him rather odd. Hannah guessed he was approaching thirty, but she didn't really know.

"Sorry, Noah," Hannah offered in return. "*Kumm* on, *kinner*, move out of the way."

The children stepped aside and stared up at Noah as he rode carefully past in his buggy.

He didn't say another word, just continued on his way.

Though she didn't say it aloud, Hannah thought to herself what a miserable man he was. Imagine shouting at three children who had just lost another parent that year, just for having a little fun in the snow.

She smiled patiently as he disappeared and then she bent down, grabbed another handful of snow, squeezed it into a ball, and launched it at Aaron.

He whooped with delight, and the snowball fight continued all the way home. For just a moment, Hannah forgot her responsibilities. She ran and played with her siblings as if she was a young teenager again. It was blissful to have ten minutes of peace, a mental respite from all her problems.

They walked up the short drive to their house still throwing snow at each other. Rachel led the way, growing bored of the game, and thinking that there might just be chocolate muffins waiting when she got inside.

She ran ahead of the others and then stopped dead in her tracks, the snow settling on her shoulder as she stood in place.

"What's that?" Rachel squealed in delight as she pointed to the stairs to the porch.

On top of the stairs, neatly wrapped in brown paper and tied with red string, was a large package.

Someone had left a gift in the snow.

CHAPTER 2

"Who is it from?" Rachel demanded, jumping up and down in delight and causing the snow to fall from his shoulders

"It has no label attached," Leah said, carefully examining the parcel. "There seems to be no address either." She looked at her older sister and raised her eyebrows. Hannah inclined her head and shrugged her shoulders as if answering an unspoken question.

"It's heavy," Aaron exclaimed, trying to pick it up but getting it no more than a few inches from the ground.

"Put it down," Hannah said quickly, trying not to snap. "Don't break it. Leah and I will carry it inside."

"I want to know who it's from," Rachel insisted. "Is it him? Did he send us a gift?"

Hannah sighed. "I have no idea."

She knew perfectly well what Rachel was referring to. It was the same silent question that Leah's raised eyes asked - the legend of the Secret Santa. It seemed ludicrous to call it that, but what better way to explain it than by using the name the *Englisch* used for the man who supposedly came down chimneys to leave gifts at Christmas time? Of course, the Amish didn't indulge in such practices. They might give small, simple gifts of a personal nature to family members. For example, Hannah had already sewn a faceless doll for Rachel this year. But there were no elaborate gifts like the *Englischers* splurged on each other, nor did they believe in the concept of Santa.

Still, for many years, something strange had happened in this Amish community.

A few days before Christmas, gifts would mysteriously appear on people's doorsteps. These gifts often went to families who had suffered hardship in the past twelve months. Sometimes it was just one gift; sometimes, a whole string of them would be left over consecutive days. Somebody, somewhere in the community, was doing a wonderful thing: bringing joy at Christmastime. For the most part, the gifts were practical items, very useful to struggling families.

Someone in the community had started calling the mystery gift giver The Secret Santa, and the name, no matter how inappropriate for an Amish community, had stuck. Even Bishop John King referred to the mystery as such.

"Is it from Secret Santa?" Aaron asked the excitement dancing in his eyes at the possibility.

"I don't know. But there's no name tag, is there? So, it must be," Hannah said, guessing that in the absence of a name tag, there could be little other explanation.

"It is! It is from Secret Santa!" Rachel squealed. "It's a Christmas miracle."

"We don't know that, little one," Leah said, ruffling her hair.

"I don't see much other explanation, do you?" Hannah asked Leah.

"I suppose not," she replied, glancing down at the parcel almost in the hope that it would reveal the identity of its sender.

They all just stood at stared at it for a few moments.

"Well, let's not stand here for the rest of the evening, staring at it. Shall we take it inside and see what it actually is?" Hannah said, excitement building in her own chest.

"*Jah!*" Rachel demanded, leaping up and down and clapping her hands in glee.

"Leah, you get that side," Hannah said, pointing to the box. "Aaron, open the door."

Hannah realized this was just the thing her siblings needed this year: a surprise gift full of wonder. She decided she would encourage the excitement.

Hannah and Leah bent down to pick up the parcel. It was heavier than Hannah expected.

"Leah, have you got a *gut* grip? Aaron, just support the middle," Hannah instructed.

After opening the door, Aaron helped his two sisters to ease the box into the kitchen, where they placed it on the table.

"What's inside? What's inside?" Rachel posed eagerly.

"Let's take our coats off and our shoes so we don't track snow everywhere," Hannah said, trying to get control of the situation.

Hannah had never seen Rachel take her shoes off so quickly before. In less than a minute, four pairs of shoes were lined up by the door, and all the coats were hung up.

"Open it, Hannah," Leah urged.

Hannah paused for a moment, wondering if there

might be something terrible inside. But she carefully untied the string and removed the brown paper, so it could be reused. Inside was a plain cardboard box, which she lifted open.

She looked down to see an array of food in front of her.

First, she pulled out bags of brightly colored candy. Four big bags. It seemed to be one for each member of the family. Aaron's eyes lit up.

"We're saving all this for Christmas, Aaron," Hannah insisted, seeing her brother's hungry eyes.

Then there was a range of general provisions: potatoes, eggs, vegetables, and cheese. These were all items Hannah had planned to purchase in the next day or so, and now there was no need.

But at the bottom, was what Hannah assumed was causing the box to be so heavy, and she could hardly believe her eyes.

She pulled out a huge side of beef, then the biggest ham she had ever seen, and finally, a turkey.

She was surprised that the box didn't break under the weight.

"We won't starve this Christmas," Leah said.

"We weren't going to starve anyway," Hannah replied, though there was a hint of relief in her voice. She had budgeted carefully so the family could enjoy some treats over the festive season, but now that budget wouldn't need to stretch so far. She certainly wouldn't have splurged on such a lavish selection of meats.

"What do you think?" Hannah asked, looking at all the gifts laid out on the table. "Has Secret Santa been kind to us?"

"He has! He has!" Rachel exclaimed.

"How do we know Secret Santa is a he?" Aaron asked, still eyeing the bags of candy, hoping his sister would relent and allow them to have at least a small taste.

"Well, we don't, I guess," Hannah said. "It could be anyone in the community."

"It is exciting," Leah said, a smile forming on her lips for the first time that afternoon. "Do you think there'll be more?"

Hannah knew the stories from previous years. Some families received multiple gifts, others just one.

She shrugged. "I think we should just be grateful, don't you?"

"Absolutely," Leah agreed.

"When we go to bed tonight and say our prayers, we must thank Secret Santa for this generosity," Hannah instructed her siblings.

Rachel nodded obediently.

"So, nobody really knows who this Secret Santa is?" Aaron asked, sitting down at the table and of course, choosing the seat closest to the candy.

Hannah scooped the candy up and moved it to a high shelf in her storage cupboard. "It's been going on for years, started probably just about the time you were born, I'm guessing."

"Can we find out who it is?" Aaron asked excitedly.

"Does it make any difference?" Leah asked.

"*Nee*, but it would be nice to thank the person, wouldn't it?" Aaron said.

Both Leah and Hannah smiled. That was their brother all over; he might be a handful at times, but deep down, he was kind and generous.

They sat in silence for a few moments. Hannah reflected on why they were receiving this special gift. They were only getting it because they had suffered this year. If she were honest, she would have preferred another family to receive the gift, sparing her siblings the pain and heartache they had endured. But she knew everything they had gone through was *Gott's* will, and there was nothing she could change. Her job now was to make life as good as possible for her three siblings.

"I'm going to put this meat away in the icehouse. Leah, I think you've got an apple strudel to finish baking, and, Aaron, no doubt you've got some homework to do. Then I'll start dinner. How does that sound?"

"Can I help with the apple strudel?" Rachel shouted, her attention now diverted.

"*Jah, kumm* on," Leah said.

The household erupted into a bustle of activity.

Later that evening, Hannah sat alone in front of the fire.

She couldn't help but to keep glancing at the window. If she were honest, the legend of Secret Santa intrigued her. She wondered who was so kind and generous as to leave such gifts. The gifts they had received today must have cost a small fortune to put together. She also wondered how many other families had received gifts this year. It was a large undertaking for someone to carry out, undetected, for all these years—nothing short of a miracle.

When she finally decided it was time for bed, she couldn't help but wonder if another gift would arrive tomorrow.

CHAPTER 3

The following day, both Hannah and Leah were busy with further preparations for Christmas. They didn't voice their thoughts out loud, but every slight noise outside had them both rushing to either the window or the door.

In the end, they both ended up bursting out laughing at the stupidity of their actions.

Despite their unspoken excitement, no further gifts came from Secret Santa.

Just like the day before, Leah accompanied Hannah to fetch the children from school. Today, there had been no further snow, and there wasn't the same boisterous fun as yesterday. But everyone was full of expectation as they walked back.

Rachel couldn't stop talking about the possibility of another gift from Secret Santa.

"I don't want you to be disappointed if we get home and there's nothing there," Hannah said. "We've received one beautiful gift and we should be very grateful. Don't you agree?"

Rachel nodded her head. "Of course."

But if Hannah was honest with herself, it wasn't just Rachel who had a look of disappointment when they returned home to find the porch bare apart from a pile of already melting snow, Hannah felt it, too.

That night as she lay in bed, she did something she hadn't done in a long time. She prayed to *Gott* for Secret Santa to come again and bring them more gifts; not for herself, of course, but because Rachel's disappointed little face earlier that day broke her heart. And it was a heart that had already been shattered once that year.

She slept deeply that night. Usually, she was the last to bed and the first to rise but this morning Leah was awake before her.

Hannah stirred, hearing Leah's footsteps in the hallway. At first, she was confused by the sounds and the soft light breaking in through the curtains. Her head was still woozy from sleep. Then she heard Leah squeal with delight.

In an instant, Hannah was out of bed. She emerged from her bedroom in just a nightdress. The front door was wide open, and Hannah took a step to the side to avoid anyone passing by on the road from seeing her in such a state.

But she could see why Leah was so delighted. At the top of the porch steps was another parcel neatly tied in brown paper and red string.

"Oh, my," Hannah said, putting a hand over her mouth. She was shocked. She genuinely thought they would receive just the one gift.

Bleary-eyed, Rachel appeared at her side. "Why is the door open?" Then she glanced outside and let out her own high-pitched squeal. That brought Aaron running from his bedroom.

"We've had another gift! Secret Santa has been back!" he shouted.

Hannah was thrilled. Her prayers had been answered. The look of delight on her siblings' faces was nothing short of wonderful.

"Can we open it?" Rachel demanded, leaping up and down in delight, just as she had when the first parcel arrived.

"Wait a minute. We all need to go in and put on

some clothes. Then we'll bring it in and open it together. Agreed?" Hannah said, assuming control once more.

Aaron and Rachel readily agreed and ran back to their bedrooms.

"I'm going to get dressed. I'll be out to help you. Do you think it's another heavy one?" Hannah asked Leah.

Leah shrugged her shoulders but smiled. "I don't know. It seems to be wrapped differently this time. I don't actually think it's in a box—just lots of brown paper."

"I'll be two minutes," Hannah said, disappearing back into her bedroom.

Before she slipped off her nightdress to change into her day clothes, she took a moment to thank *Gott* for answering her prayer. A part of her felt guilty for asking for gifts for her family, it felt selfish somehow. But she was grateful, not for the material things, but for the joy that the whole process brought to her younger siblings. They needed some joy in their young lives.

She quickly dressed and reemerged into the hallway. Rachel and Aaron were already there, demanding that Leah carry the parcel inside. Leah tried picking it up and found it much lighter than the previous one. She managed it on her own and carefully brought it to the kitchen table. Snow had obviously fallen earlier that morning, and there was a light dusting on top of the brown parcel. Leah brushed it away casually with her hands.

"Why don't you open this one, Rachel," Hannah said, gently lifting Rachel so that she was standing on one of the kitchen chairs, now almost the same height as Hannah.

"Take care not to rip it," Leah whispered as her younger sister started unwrapping the parcel.

One of the key lessons Hannah had managed to teach Leah since their mother's passing three years ago was the need to be frugal. Items like brown paper and string could be used in countless ways around the household. In many ways, they were like an extra gift.

Despite her excitement, Rachel did exactly as she was told. She carefully folded the brown paper to reveal yet another practical gift. This time, it was items of warm outdoor clothing. A set for each member of the family. Scarves that appeared to be hand-knitted, matching gloves, and brand-new outdoor coats. The coats were thick and heavy, and Hannah knew perfectly well they must've cost a small fortune. It seemed like a miracle that each item was the right size for its recipient. A handwritten label on each in exquisite calligraphy named its intended recipient: Rachel, Aaron, Leah, and Hannah. And finally, at the bottom of the package were four pairs of woolen socks for wearing around the house.

Aaron pulled on his coat and marveled at how grown-up it made him look.

Hannah let out a sigh of relief. Aaron had almost outgrown his current winter coat, and he was still far too small to wear their father's coat. It was an item Hannah had refused to give away after his death. If the winter had been harsh this year, she had been fully expecting to have to buy her brother a new coat. Now, she wouldn't have to.

It was almost as if Secret Santa knew exactly what the family needed.

Hannah pulled on her own coat and wrapped the beautifully knitted black scarf around her neck.

"Beautiful, aren't they?" she said to Leah, who was doing the same with her own garments.

"Can I wear it to school?" Rachel asked eagerly.

"After Christmas. We'll save it for our best until then," Hannah said.

Rachel's face looked a little disappointed, and Hannah felt guilty for dampening her sibling's joy, even if just for a second. But she knew she was being practical. Rachel had a perfectly good winter coat for now, and it made sense for her to wear that one to school, where there was a greater chance it might get damaged. This new coat could be saved for a special occasion. Besides, it was a little big, so Rachel had plenty of time to grow into it.

It was almost as if Secret Santa knew what was needed in the household and had even allowed for the rapid growth of a small child.

As he carefully removed the new coat to hang it up, Aaron said something that made Hannah think.

"I wish I knew who the Secret Santa was so I could thank them."

CHAPTER 4

*L*ater that morning, Hannah was out in town alone. The two youngest children were in school, and Leah had gone to visit some of her friends for coffee and cake before Christmas. Leah felt guilty taking the money from Hannah to pay for it, but Hannah smiled and insisted.

"We're doing okay," she said as she placed $10 in her sibling's hand and closed her fist around it. "You need to enjoy your life too."

Leah smiled softly back. "Just remember that you do as well, Hannah. Amish women your age are starting to court."

Hannah knew Leah was a complex character. At times, she was full of typical teenage impulses. But in moments like this, it almost seemed as if their mother was speaking when Leah spoke.

"There will be plenty of time for that," Hannah insisted.

Leah nodded, but Hannah could immediately see the doubt in her eyes.

In many ways, Leah spoke the truth. Hannah had no time to go to the Sunday singings, where young, single Amish people typically met to socialize and maybe find romance. She had a household to run and three siblings to raise. She wasn't going to shirk her responsibilities by running off in a vain attempt to court boys. All of that could come later in life. There was no rush; she was, after all, only eighteen. Although, she would turn nineteen in early January.

The snow had started falling yet again, and Hannah was grateful for her brand-new coat and the beautiful scarf she tightened around her neck.

"Hello, Hannah. How are you doing?" a voice said in front of her.

Hannah had been lost in thought, thinking about Leah's words earlier that day. Yes, she would soon be nineteen, but she honestly felt a lot older. Maybe her sister was right, maybe she did need to make time for herself. And yes, maybe that did include court- ing. But she brushed it off, how many young Amish men would want to get involved in bringing up three siblings? She didn't know the answer, but she guessed it wasn't many. Hannah looked up to see the voice belonged to Naomi Bender. She was an elderly Amish widow. Hannah didn't really know her age, but she guessed her to be in her late seventies. Naomi smiled at her with kind eyes.

"I'm very well, *danke*, Naomi. How are you?" Hannah replied with a smile in return.

"It's Christmas season. You know what it's like. Very busy," Naomi said.

Naomi had miraculously raised fourteen children during the course of her long marriage. Her husband had died only two years ago, and she felt his loss greatly. Amazingly, she now boasted 39 grandchildren and five great-grandchildren. Despite her age, her memory was as sharp as a tack, and she could name them all effortlessly.

"Is that a new coat, Hannah? Didn't you used to have a blue one?" Naomi asked, pulling the detail from the back of her mind.

Hannah glanced down at the beautiful, yet simple black coat and couldn't help but reach out with her left hand to touch its softness and warmth.

"*Jah*, it is." She glanced around and took a small step forward. She lowered her voice, forcing Naomi to step closer so they huddled together. "It's a gift from Secret Santa," she said, uttering the words almost guilty as though spoiling a great surprise. But at the same time, she didn't want Naomi to think she was splurging on gifts for herself.

"Oh, I see," Naomi said, her eyes lighting up. "That's delightful, isn't it?"

A sudden thought struck Hannah. Since her husband's death, Naomi had thrown herself into community life. She had restarted the quilting circle that had faded away in recent years. Of course, it was called a quilting circle, but when the group met once a week, it wasn't just quilts they made. Some of them knitted, and Hannah had heard stories that Naomi Bender was probably the best knitter in the entire community.

Naomi's husband had run a very successful business in his time. Hannah was sure the older woman had no financial concerns. Could it be that she was Secret Santa? Had she started it years ago, and just continued the practice? There seemed to be a twinkle of excitement in Naomi's eyes when Hannah mentioned the fact that the coat was a gift from Secret Santa.

"I got this scarf and gloves too, all beautifully knitted," Hannah said in a conspiratorial tone. "As did my siblings, of course. They must have been made by someone very skilled."

"It is fine work," Naomi said in an almost embarrassed voice.

"I don't suppose you know anything about who's sending the gifts, Naomi? My siblings and I would love to thank them," Hannah asked, ensuring she held Naomi's gaze. After a moment of uncomfortable silence, Naomi glanced to the ground and shook her head.

"*Nee*, I know nothing about it other than the fact it's a beautiful gesture," Naomi replied as though she had considered her answer. "Anyway, I must be off. As I said, Christmas is always a busy time of the year with all these grandchildren to feed. They all want a slice of fruitcake." She laughed. "I don't know where they put it all!"

Hannah laughed along at the joke, said her farewells, and watched the old woman shuffle off.

"Take care in the snow," Hannah called after her.

As Naomi disappeared down the road, Hannah wondered: Could it be that Naomi Bender was Secret Santa? She had seemed very evasive when the question was asked. It was a possibility, surely.

But then Hannah realized something. The earlier food parcel had been extremely heavy. It had taken both her and Leah, with a little help from Aaron as well, to get the parcel inside. There was no way Naomi could have lifted that alone.

But then she thought of Naomi's fourteen children. Eight of them were sons. Four of them were farmers. Huge men with seemingly endless strength.

Maybe Naomi had enlisted one or more of them to help in her little game.

It was certainly a possibility.

Hannah smiled to herself. It would be fun to discover who the Secret Santa really was. Maybe they could turn the tables and provide a little gift of their own. Leah made some wonderful chocolate muffins; maybe a small batch of those would be a special treat for Secret Santa. Hannah nodded, pleased with her idea.

But, of course, she had to uncover the identity of Secret Santa first. The question remained: Was Naomi Bender the Secret Santa, or were there other possibilities?

CHAPTER 5

*L*eah was very excited when she met Hannah after having coffee and cake with her friends. She had news to share.

Apparently, Secret Santa had been busy throughout the community. Her friends were aware of at least two other families that had benefited recently from Secret Santa's generosity.

The Schrock family, with six young children, had apparently received a package of warm winter blankets. The family had suffered a devastating fire just before harvest season, and their barn and much of the crop had been destroyed.

The Schmucker family had also been given a package of food along with a small sum of money, although Leah didn't know how much. They had endured hardship earlier in the year when their buggy, which was parked at the side of the road, was crashed into by an *Englisch* car. Fortunately, all the members of the family were safe. However, their family horse had to be put down by the vet.

Hannah was pleased to hear that others in their community were also receiving gifts.

Hannah explained her plan to her sister. They would try to identify who was behind the Secret Santa mystery within the community so they could present this person with their own little gift in return.

"We probably don't want to spoil the magic by revealing it, though, if we do find out," Leah said.

Once again, Hannah heard her own mother's words in Leah's voice.

"*Nee*, you're right, of course; we don't. Maybe if we do discover who it is, we don't tell Aaron and Rachel. They probably wouldn't be able to hold their tongues."

Leah voiced her agreement and was soon listing the names of possible suspects. Hannah couldn't help but smile at her enthusiasm.

Approaching the store in town, they saw Anna Riehl standing outside, holding a pot to collect money for the poorer of the town's inhabitants.

The town was an interesting place. The vast majority of the residents were Amish, but probably a quarter were *Englischers*. Many other *Englischers* came from the surrounding areas to purchase goods from the Amish shops. Especially over Christmastime, items like Amish furniture, quilts, and baked goods were particularly valued by the *Englisch*. At times like Christmas, charity collections took place, and it didn't matter if people were Amish or *Englisch*, they helped where they could.

Hannah felt she really must contribute to the cause, especially considering her family's good fortune.

"Morning, Hannah. Morning, Leah," Anna greeted with a smile. "It's nice to see you."

She pulled out a $5 bill and walked up to the woman. Hannah bent over and was about to put the money into the pot when Anna's hand immediately covered it. She shook her head and lowered her voice.

"I appreciate the gesture, Hannah, I truly do. But keep it."

Hannah stood up, a little shocked. She looked at Anna, who smiled back.

A thought suddenly hit her as she stood looking at the older woman. Could Anna be the Secret

Santa? This was exactly the sort of thing she did regularly, standing outside, no matter the weather, collecting money for those less fortunate than herself. Hannah guessed she was in her fifties although people always said that Anna had aged well. There was no doubt she was still a beautiful woman. She was married and had one daughter who had long since married and now lived with her own husband. Anna's husband was a successful farmer who employed many members of the community, and even some *Englischers* to help in his fields. It seemed highly plausible that Anna could be the one leaving the gifts. She wondered how she neither she nor Leah had mentioned her name a few moments ago. They both knew how much work Anna did for the community. Of course, there were none of the problems that Naomi Bender might have had with being the Secret Santa. With her husband's assistance, carrying heavy parcels wouldn't be an issue. Knowing Anna for many years, it would be just the sort of thing Hannah could imagine her finding entertaining.

Hannah decided to test her with a few questions. "*Nee*, we insist, Anna. Please. We've been blessed with some *gut* fortune over the past few days. Secret

Santa has visited us not once, but twice. We are unbelievably grateful, aren't we, Leah?"

"We are indeed," Leah said, smiling at her sister. "We all received brand-new coats just this morning." Leah reached out her arm as if to prove her point to Anna.

Hannah studied the older woman closely, looking for anything that might give her away. Anna smiled warmly.

"That is wonderful news. I'm so pleased for you all," she said. But despite the words, there seemed to be nothing else behind her eyes. "You all deserve it."

"So, I'd really like to give something back. It's only a small offering," Hannah said, folding up the $5 bill once more.

Anna considered the gesture for a moment and then removed her hand. It was clear she didn't want to hurt Hannah and Leah's pride. "*Danke*, you are both so kind."

Hannah nodded. "We're just giving back a little of our own *gut* fortune, that's all. What I'd really like to do is to thank Secret Santa personally. I have to say, the gifts we've received over the last few days have really lit up our lives, especially for Aaron and little Rachel."

Anna smiled and nodded but gave no further response.

Hannah decided to push a little more. "I don't suppose you might be Secret Santa? You seem like the sort of person who would do something like this."

Anna laughed loudly. "I agree, it's *Wunderbar*. I like to do my bit, but I don't have time for such secrets. I don't like being out at night, for one thing. Not these days."

Hannah sensed no dishonesty in Anna's reply and nodded.

"We'd better go get our grocery shopping done," Hannah said to Leah. "Thank you for everything you do, Anna. I know the community certainly appreciates it."

"*Danke*, Hannah, that's such a kind and considerate thing to say," Anna said, looking close to tears at Hannah's kind words. "Thank you again for your donation," she added.

Hannah and Leah walked into the grocery store. "Did you really think it was her?" Leah asked.

Hannah shrugged, now unsure. "It could easily have been. Think of all the work she does for the community."

"I thought she seemed a little shocked when you

asked," Leah replied, shaking her head. "I don't think it's her."

"Maybe not," Hannah said. "But it must be someone."

Over the next half an hour, she pushed the thought of the Secret Santa out of her mind. She had her grocery shopping to do. The arrival of the first parcel a few days ago meant that they had less to buy, which meant less expenditure, which was a weight off her mind.

Just as they were finishing their shopping, an Amish man rushed past them, snatching items quickly off the shelves as he went. They weren't looking and didn't catch who he was as he went by

At the checkout, the friendly young *Englisch* cashier was chatting away as the man packed his groceries. Hannah and Leah were next in line behind him, and they recognized him as Noah Beiler, the strange man who had shouted at them on the way home from school a few days ago.

He didn't look at Hannah or Leah, or even at the cashier who was trying to engage him in conversation. He just grabbed his groceries and packed them as quickly as was humanly possible.

"So, what are your plans for Christmas then?" she asked as he handed over his money.

He mumbled a response that Hannah couldn't quite make out before he hurried out the door, leaving the *Englisch* shaking her head.

"Did I say something wrong?" the young woman asked Hannah.

Hannah knew the woman was new to working in the store. The last time she had come to do her shopping, it had been her first day and she was undergoing training.

"Don't worry," Hannah laughed, looking at the perplexed cashier. "He's always like that. He's well-known throughout the community for being…"

She stopped speaking as she tried to think of a suitable word, finally, Leah finished her sentence for her "…odd."

Hannah shot her younger sister a quick look that suggested she shouldn't really be saying such things about an older member of their community. But then, all three of them broke out into small ripples of laughter. The cashier was relieved that she hadn't said anything out of place, because she was new to working in the store and hadn't had much interaction with the Amish up until now.

"He's certainly short on Christmas spirit," she said to Leah as she set about scanning their items.

Hannah watched Noah Beiler loading his shopping into his buggy outside, and she saw him pointing at something and shaking his head. He was obviously having a disagreement with someone. She decided that they would avoid him on the way out.

Maybe he could do with a visit from Secret Santa to lighten his mood.

CHAPTER 6

The next morning, Hannah was awake first. After dressing and emerging from her bedroom, the first thing she did was open the front door.

There was nothing there.

Her heart sank a little. She knew she had already received two wonderful gifts, but the excitement of the possibility of more had captured her. Then she felt guilty for that brief moment of disappointment when she saw nothing but a fresh dusting of snow on the porch step. She would try to do better in the future and be more grateful for what they had.

She went to the kitchen and proceeded to prepare breakfast. Eggs on toast was the staple breakfast food for them each morning. It was simple, hearty, and, above all, a cheap way to start the day.

She heard each of her siblings rise in turn and couldn't help but laugh when the first thing any of them did was walk to the front door and open it.

"No gifts," Rachel said in a slightly forlorn voice when she came into the kitchen.

"And *Gut* Morning to you as well, Rachel," Hannah said in a half rebuke of the little girl for not saying good morning. "We've had many gifts, though, haven't we? *Gott* has blessed us this Christmas season. We will be grateful for what we've got."

Rachel nodded meekly and took her place at the kitchen table. "*Jah,* Hannah. I'm sorry."

Twenty minutes later, the siblings had all finished breakfast. Hannah was getting her boots on to take Aaron and Rachel to school. She had no doubt there would be a last-minute rush when one of them discovered that they had forgotten something.

Leah was also preparing to leave the house. She was going to the bishop's house with a group of young people. They were going to make preparations for the traditional Amish caroling that would take place in town just before Christmas. Hannah was pleased that her sister had decided to get involved in this project. It was a way for them to give back a little to the community, especially after recent events. It was also good for her to be more social in the community. Leah still saw her friends after leaving school, but after the death of their father, she had become slightly more withdrawn from community events, making excuses of illness so she didn't have to attend. Hannah did have worries about her younger sister. She heard story after story from communities the length of the country of young people leaving the Amish. She worried that Leah's withdrawal from community events might be a sign of her questioning her faith. Helping to arrange the caroling was a great way for her to get more involved.

Half an hour later, Hannah had walked the two youngest siblings to school and had hurried home, her mind still preoccupied with Christmas preparations and all that still needed to be done around the house. She always liked to do a deep clean, just like her mother had done before the festivities. There was nothing better than a nice, good clean before Christmas. If things went according to plan, she would do that tomorrow. But today, she had to take advantage of the fact that Leah would be out of the house. She had a collection to make in town.

She rushed home and was about to hitch up the buggy when she caught sight of the front step of the porch. While she was walking up the drive, she had failed to notice it, but now she saw it clearly. A white envelope that was perched on top of the dusting of snow.

There was writing on the front, in the same beautiful calligraphy that had been on the labels of the coats.

It simply said: The Fishers.

She picked it up and knew instantly it was from Secret Santa; the writing told her that. She was slightly shocked that something more had arrived for them that day. Hannah considered for a moment whether she should wait for her siblings to return but decided against it. She gently opened the envelope, taking care not to tear it. She almost fell over with shock. Inside were crisp $50 bills, ten of them.

She gasped in disbelief and put a hand to her mouth. On top of everything else, this was staggering.

Hannah was slightly embarrassed. Who was

Secret Santa that he or she or they thought her family needed so much help? She felt hurt, wondering if maybe Secret Santa thought she wasn't coping very well with raising her siblings. Maybe they felt her family needed all this assistance to keep them going. She shook her head and decided to go inside.

She sat down at the kitchen table and counted the bills again as if somehow the number might change. As she did so, she noticed her hands shaking with the shock.

Then her thoughts drifted back to yesterday when Anna had tried to persuade Hannah not to contribute to her collection. Could this be her reward for doing so? Maybe Anna was Secret Santa after all, paying back Hannah's contribution a hundredfold?

She wondered what she would tell her siblings. She decided she would probably tell Leah the full truth but settled on telling Aaron and Rachel they had received some money. They probably wouldn't understand the concept of $500 or how meaningful it was. That money could keep the household running well into spring, especially with the other gifts they had received, and Hannah's diligent budgeting for the festivities.

Suddenly, she realized the time and remembered her appointment in town. She quickly hid the money in an old, battered tin, placing it high on a shelf behind the candy that had arrived in the first gift.

She rushed out of the house, hitched up the buggy, and headed to town. She had a growing sense of unease as she got closer to the center. She looked up at the sky and thought it looked to carry the threat of snow.

Just as she arrived at her destination, the heavens opened, and snow fell like she hadn't seen in years. She had an appointment at the fabric shop where she was to collect three lengths of fabric to gift to Leah for Christmas. She hadn't received a new dress in at least eighteen months, and it was high time Leah stopped repairing the old ones and made new ones. Hannah had already made an appointment with Ruth Miller who ran the shop, and the fabric she'd selected was waiting for her.

After a quick exchange of pleasantries and some gossip about the gifts being received throughout the community, Hannah once more expressed her gratitude for what they'd been given. Although she made no mention of the money she had received today, slightly embarrassed as she was by the generosity that had been shown to her.

"As it's getting bad out there, you had better get going, Hannah," Ruth said, looking out the window. "Let me help you to the buggy."

The two women left the shop and almost bumped into Gideon Zook. "Oh, my, where are you going in such a rush?" Gideon asked.

Gideon was seventy years old, with a long white beard and a completely bald head; not that anyone could see it today, underneath his hat, which in turn was now covered by the heavy snow. Despite his age, Gideon was as strong as an ox and still got involved in every single barn raising.

"Sorry, Gideon," Hannah said quickly, opening the buggy and putting the fabric inside where it would be safe. "Are you okay?"

"Quite well, *danke*, Hannah. No one would want to hear if I wasn't," he said, with humor in his voice. "And how is Ruth? How's business?"

"*Jah*, I'm very well, *danke*, Gideon. Business is *gut*. It is Christmas after all," Ruth replied. "But if you don't mind, I should get inside, out of this snow."

Gideon nodded. Ruth thanked Hannah once again for her custom and disappeared inside her shop, kicking the snow from her shoes before she entered.

"Are you heading home, Gideon?" Hannah asked the older man.

"I am, especially now that this weather has turned."

"Would you like me to give you a lift in the buggy?" Hannah offered. Gideon lived on her route home, and it wouldn't be out of her way. It seemed like the obvious, kind thing to do, given the circumstances.

"That would be very kind of you. *Jah*, I would appreciate that greatly," Gideon said, climbing up into the buggy. Hannah ran around the other side, waving to Ruth who was watching them from the window.

She automatically flicked the switch that turned on the heater inside the buggy. It was connected to the same battery that operated the lights at the back. It was another allowance made in recent years. Thankfully, Bishop John King understood the need for progress.

"It gets quite toasty in here, doesn't it?" Gideon said after a few seconds. He laughed as though he didn't altogether approve.

"*Jah*, I'm glad for it during the winter months," Hannah replied.

"How are you coping this Christmas season with everything?" Gideon asked softly.

There was a sudden sadness in Hannah's chest as she realized, yet again, that this would be their first Christmas without their beloved father.

"We're coping, *danke*, Gideon," she replied. She decided to change the topic of conversation. "We've been blessed."

"How so?" Gideon asked.

"I don't know if you've heard, but we've been getting a few gifts from Secret Santa."

Gideon laughed. "Oh, that is *wunderbar* news! Secret Santa—such a funny name, so worldly, isn't it? Wouldn't have been allowed back when I was a young *mann*, of course." He paused for a moment, then eyed Hannah with a curious look. "I'm glad it's allowed these days, though. *Wunderbar* initiative."

Hannah grinned. Gideon was a man without family. He'd been married 40 years ago but had suffered a great tragedy when his wife died in childbirth two years later. The man had never remarried.

"Do you know anything about who Secret Santa might be, Gideon?" Hannah asked suddenly.

This was a man who lived alone, but despite his age, she knew how strong he was. She had watched him lift huge planks of wood at a barn raising just that summer with effortless ease. The only reason she had offered to give him a lift was because of the heavy snow, not because he was frail. She knew he could have easily lifted the heavy food parcel they received the other day.

"One of the things I don't get involved in is gossip," Gideon said with a laugh.

"So, no idea at all?" Hannah persisted.

"Not something I've ever considered, Hannah, to be honest." He gave her a look that suggested the matter was closed and that such gossip was, in his eyes, sinful.

Hannah couldn't help but smile to herself. His comments were funny in a way. He was, after all, an older gentleman, and the community had evolved a bit more than he might be comfortable with.

For the rest of the journey to his house, they talked about other matters, the caroling service coming up, Aaron's schooling, and the opportunities the New Year might bring.

When they arrived at his house, Gideon thanked Hannah for her kindness.

"I'm glad you've been blessed with the gifts, Hannah. You deserve it. It's a wonderful thing you're doing, raising your siblings. Your parents would be so proud."

Hannah muttered a quick reply and thanks and moved the buggy forward.

Although she heard similar sentiments on a regular basis, Gideon's words resonated with her, and she couldn't help but let a tear fall from her eye.

CHAPTER 7

$\mathcal{T}$en minutes after leaving Gideon, tears were still flowing down Hannah's face. Something in the tone of his voice had really hit home for her. The grief and the stress of the last few years and more specifically the last few months were now finally coming out. She had been forced to be strong for the sake of her siblings. There was no other choice. But now it seemed there was a flood of emotion that Hannah seemed unable to contain.

"Your parents would be so proud."

The words echoed around her head, again, again and again.

She sincerely hoped that they were, but she thought she was failing on so many levels.

Would her parents really be proud?

What about that time she had shouted at Rachel for losing her shoes? Or snapped at Aaron for playing outside when he should have been digging in the vegetable bed?

The salty tears that filled her eyes, coupled with the relentless snow, blinded her. Her head was so full of her faults and the mistakes she had made since her mother's passing that she didn't notice her surroundings. The horse plowed on through the driving snow, taking Hannah homeward.

Suddenly, there was a blinding flash of light and the sound of a horn blasting.

Hannah was jolted from her thoughts and thrust back into reality. Her heart raced and the anxiety grew even further in her chest.

An *Englisch* car was heading straight toward her. She pulled hard on the reins to the right, realizing she was all over the road. The car brushed past her with only inches to spare, its horn sounding the driver's discontent at her road usage.

The panic that had filled her body slowly subsided as she regained control of her emotions. But the horse veered off to the side of the road and, without warning, there was a small thud. The horse tried to move forward, but the buggy wouldn't budge.

She sat for almost a full minute, collecting herself. Her pulse slowed and her breathing shallowed as she forced herself to calm down. She pushed Gideon's words and all thoughts that she was a failure to the back of her mind.

Now she had a new problem to solve.

Glancing out to the side, she saw that she had foolishly managed to guide the buggy into a snowdrift. The wheels on one side were stuck firmly in the snow.

Now that she understood the situation, she once again felt like crying. This shouldn't be happening.

Then the words of her father came to her: "In winter, always have a shovel in the back of the buggy," her father had told her from an early age.

And that's exactly what she had done. On October 1st, she had placed a shovel safely in the back. She had never known snow in these areas until at least December, but her motto was "Better safe than sorry."

She knew she had little choice, and there was just one option, she had to get out into the snowstorm and dig the buggy out of the snow. She was grateful for her new coat, scarf, and gloves. They would offer her some protection.

Turning around, she reached into the back to

find that the shovel was still there, just where she had left it. She grabbed it and jumped out of the buggy to land thigh-deep in snow. She gasped in shock; she hadn't expected it to be so deep. Each step was a struggle. She moved to the front wheel and began digging.

After two shovelfuls, she was already exhausted. Digging snow was no easy task. Her shoulders and back screamed in protest, but she knew she had to keep going. She had to work quickly. Glancing at the other side of the buggy, she saw that snow was already building up around those wheels, too.

If she wasn't careful, she would become trapped out here.

"Let me help," a voice came from behind her.

She turned, amazed to see Noah Beiler standing there. Even more surprisingly, he was dressed in just pants, a shirt, and a hat. He seemed untroubled by the weather. She wondered where he had come from but guessed she might be near his house. The snow was falling so heavily that it was almost impossible to see where she was.

"Noah?" Hannah said, confused - not only by his presence and state of dress but also by his willing-ness to help.

He took two steps forward and gently pried the

shovel from her hands. He worked quickly and tirelessly.

"Go back inside the buggy, out of the snow," he muttered, not even looking at her.

After a moment of hesitation and considering his strange behavior, she climbed back into the buggy. The warmth from the heater was welcome. The bottom half of her legs were now soaked from the ice-cold snow.

In a little over five minutes, Noah had cleared the snow.

He reached out and handed the shovel back to Hannah. "Will you be okay getting home?" he asked in his gruff voice. He looked almost comical, dressed in just shirt sleeves and with at least an inch of snow on top of his hat.

Hannah nodded. "*Jah*, it's just a quarter of a mile. I'm sure I'll be fine. *Danke* for your help. I appreciate it so much, Noah."

Noah nodded but stood silent.

Was there something else in his expression? Was that a hint of a smile? Hannah didn't have time to study him any longer because, as suddenly as he had appeared, he was gone, disappearing into the white snowstorm. She stared at the empty space for just a moment before picking up the reins and moving the horse forward. The last thing she needed was to linger here too long and get stuck again.

It took fifteen minutes to cover the short distance back home. When she saw the turn into the driveway, she felt nothing but relief.

If it hadn't been for Noah, the buggy might have been stuck out there all night. She would have to think of a way to thank him.

She quickly unhitched the buggy and led her horse to the safety and warmth of the stables.

Then she retrieved the fabric she had bought from Ruth and took it inside. After considering several places to store it, she hid it under her bed. She would wrap it before Christmas.

After getting out of her wet clothes, she decided on a comforting mug of hot coffee.

As she made it, she realized her hands were shaking. The flashing lights of the *Englisch* car and the blast of its horn replayed in her mind.

A fresh horror hit her. She realized she could have been killed out there today. And then what would have happened to her siblings?

She had to be more careful.

A few sips of the warm chocolate settled her nerves, and her thoughts drifted back to Noah, digging her buggy out of the snow. She knew so little about him. He lived alone, was unmarried, and rarely mingled. She wondered what had happened in his life to make him this way. Why didn't he integrate into the community a little more?

His gruff nature clearly didn't endear him to people. Take the incident where he shouted at the children the other day. There was no real need for that. Or the rudeness he displayed in the store. It was strange the way he behaved. Despite the fact that Leah shouldn't have said what she did, she was right, Noah Beiler was odd.

But today, she couldn't have been more grateful to him.

CHAPTER 8

*T*hat night, Leah nearly fell off her chair when Hannah told her how much money they had received from Secret Santa

She shared with the rest of the family that they had received another gift, only after the children got home from school. She explained it was money, which she had put away for safekeeping, but she showed the two children the beautifully written envelope.

Neither of the two asked about the amount.

Hannah found that rather comforting. They were just pleased to have received another gift and weren't concerned about how much it was worth.

"That will last us for months, won't it?" Leah said

softly, staring at the notes her sister had laid out on the kitchen table.

Hannah nodded. "It certainly will."

"It must be someone with considerable wealth doing all this," Leah said.

"That was my thought, too. I have to admit, my mind went straight to Anna. Doesn't it seem odd that we received a gift of money so soon after making a donation yesterday?" Hannah asked her sister.

Leah thought back to the incident outside the store in town, where Anna had initially refused to take Hannah's money. "Possibly. Maybe she's trying to repay your kindness."

"That was my thought as well. Still, it could be anyone, really. I know Naomi and Gideon both denied it, but it could easily be them."

"I doubt it could be Naomi. Remember, some of our gifts have been heavy. She would definitely need help if it were her. But Gideon could've lifted the box of food without any trouble."

Hannah gathered the money and put it back in the tin. "So, what we're saying is, we're no closer to discovering who the Secret Santa is."

"I guess not," Leah agreed.

"Maybe it's better that way," Hannah said. "Maybe it would spoil the mystery if we found out."

"But, as you say, it would be nice to do something for them if we did manage to find out." Leah countered.

That night, they went to bed, both tossing and turning as they considered the potential persons of interest. By the time they woke the next day, they were no closer to solving the mystery.

The next morning, they woke to another heavy blanket of snow. Today was the day of the carol singing in town. Leah mentioned how the preparations with the bishop had gone well yesterday. The entire family would go down and take part. Hannah knew it would be difficult for her personally. This was something they had done every year with their parents, but this year would be the first time they'd do it without the two of them.

Around the home, preparations for Christmas were in full swing. Today, Hannah would cook the large ham they received from Secret Santa. They would eat it warm for dinner with simple mashed potatoes, and there would be plenty left cold for the rest of the festive season.

Leah continued her baking, making sure there

were plenty of the sweet treats that Aaron and Rachel loved so much.

As the snow continued to fall, Hannah happened to glance out the kitchen window.

"*Ach, nee*!" she exclaimed in dismay.

"What's the matter?" Leah asked, joining her sister and wiping flour from her hands.

"The fence finally collapsed," Hannah pointed out the window.

The fence to the left of the driveway had been getting more and more unstable since the summer. It was the kind of job Hannah wasn't skilled at. It was really man's work, and Aaron was too young to help. Although they managed small repairs around the house as needed, she had been putting off hiring someone to do the work.

"It was bound to collapse eventually, wasn't it?" Leah said.

"The *gut* news is, we now have the money from Secret Santa. It won't cost that much to fix, of course," Hannah said, putting on a positive voice. It was a pain, and she didn't really want the hassle, but it was a job that needed doing now.

School was finishing early that day, as it was the final day before the Christmas holidays. That way, everyone could get home, be fed, and get ready for caroling in town that evening.

The two children were full of typical Christmas excitement as they walked home. Their immediate chatter was about Secret Santa, wondering if more gifts had arrived today. Hannah assured them there hadn't been. Aaron entertained himself by running about 20 yards ahead, leaping into the biggest snowdrifts he could find. After the first two, Hannah had given up scolding him. His school clothes would need washing anyway, and she would instruct him to bathe that afternoon, so what harm could it do?

He ran around the corner toward home. Moments later, he returned with a look of confusion on his face.

"There's a *mann* repairing our fence," Aaron said, walking up to Hannah.

Hannah glanced at Leah, who shook her head to indicate her own confusion. They turned the corner and walked the last few yards to the driveway. Aaron was right, there was a man repairing the fence. Though his back was turned, Hannah immediately recognized him.

Despite the snow covering the ground, the man was dressed only in pants, shirt sleeves, and a hat.

She knew, even before they approached him, who it was. It was Noah.

"Noah?" Hannah called out as she got closer.

He just turned and grunted in response.

"What are you doing?" Hannah asked, genuinely confused about how he came to be repairing the fence.

"I was passing by, saw the fence was down, and thought I'd fix it for you," he said in the same gruff voice he'd used when digging her buggy out of the snow just the other day.

"That's awfully kind of you, but there was no need," Hannah said, almost embarrassed.

"Just helping, that's all," Noah said, turning back to his task and swinging his large hammer to drive the fence post into the ground.

Hannah and the rest of the family watched him for a moment. "*Kumm* on, let's get everyone inside," Hannah said in the direction of Leah. "*Danke*, Noah, I really do appreciate it," she added as she ushered the children into the house.

"That was very nice of him to do," Leah said after they had taken off their shoes.

The aroma of ham filled the air. Aaron was already rummaging for food.

"Wait until lunch," Hannah instructed, pointing

her finger at the boy who had already opened the cupboard door. "Go and get changed: you'll catch your death of cold in those wet clothes."

He didn't argue and did as his sister told him.

Rachel went off to play with her dolls in front of the fire.

"I forgot to tell you; yesterday, I got the buggy stuck in the snow, and Noah suddenly appeared out of nowhere and helped dig me out. Now he's here, fixing the fence," Hannah told her younger sister in hushed tones.

Leah laughed. "Maybe he's got a soft spot for you, Hannah."

Hannah's eyes widened. "I wouldn't have thought so."

The two women stood for a moment, watching Noah work. It seemed odd that he wasn't even wearing a coat in the freezing weather, but it didn't seem to bother him in the slightest. Whenever he swung the heavy hammer to drive the fence post home, Hannah saw his arms bulge. He seemed to do it with effortless ease. There was no doubting Noah was a strong man.

"I'll make him a cup of *kaffe*, it's the least we can do," Hannah said, moving toward the row of clean mugs lined up on the sideboard.

CHAPTER 9

en minutes later, Hannah was stepping out into the snow. She wasn't brave enough to venture outside without a coat. Besides, she had to cover up the large wet patch down the side of her dress caused during the disaster with one of her old pans, the one she knew had a very loose handle. Fortunately, the water had been cold. It wasn't the only cooking implement that had seen better days.

After Christmas, she thought, a good use of some of the Secret Santa money could be the purchase of a new set of cookware and maybe some new knives.

"Here we go, Noah. I brought you this," Hannah said as she approached the man.

He turned and looked almost shocked to see her standing there, arm outstretched with a mug of steaming hot coffee.

He studied her for a moment and then put down the hammer.

"*Danke*, Hannah. That's kind of you," Noah said, his voice losing some of its usual gruffness. He stepped towards her and took the warm coffee cup from her hands, cradling it as if it were a small child.

He gave Hannah a soft smile after taking his first sip. She watched him, recognizing an unnoticed endearing quality about him. He was also strangely handsome. He seemed genuinely surprised by her act of kindness.

"It's the least I could do. Oh! I almost forgot," she said, reaching into her pocket and pulling out a neatly wrapped cinnamon roll. "I have this as well."

Noah's eyes grew wide with wonder as she held out the baked delicacy, almost as if he hadn't seen anything like it before.

"*Danke*."

Hannah giggled softly. "I don't know why you're thanking me. You're the one out here fixing my fence in a snowstorm. It's me who should thank you! It's just a cup of *kaffe* and a cinnamon roll, though I have to admit it's not my baking. My *schweschder*, Leah is the one who made it."

"Tastes *gut*," Noah said, then quickly tried to remember his manners, realizing he was speaking with his mouth full.

"She'll be pleased," Hannah said, half-laughing, genuinely delighted that Noah seemed to appreciate her small offering.

"Why are you out here in just your shirt sleeves? It was the same yesterday when you dug me out of the snow. Don't you have a coat?"

Noah shrugged. "I'm not sure, really. I don't think I feel the cold, that's all. I can't remember the last time I wore a coat, to be honest."

They stood in silence for a few seconds. Hannah realized that Noah wasn't much of a conversationalist, even though this was the most she'd ever managed to get out of him.

"Are you going to the caroling tonight in town?"

"Is that tonight?" Noah asked, looking back at the fence post he'd just hammered in.

"*Jah*, everyone will be there. You should go," Hannah said.

"I probably will," Noah said, gently tapping on the top of the fence post with his free hand as if he wasn't convinced it was level. But Hannah knew perfectly well that his answer was a lie. Noah rarely showed up at community events. While he attended some Sunday services, she couldn't recall seeing him at a wedding or a community meal. Not that she had been looking for him, of course, but for some reason, she doubted he'd be there.

She wondered how a man like Noah managed on his own. "Do you cook for yourself, Noah?" she asked.

Noah looked at her as if the question were strange. "What do you mean?"

Hannah remembered the way he'd looked at the cinnamon roll Leah had baked, devouring it as if he were ravenous. He was a big, strong man with broad shoulders and a wide chest, so surely, he must eat plenty.

"You live on your own. Do you cook your own meals?"

"I get by, Hannah. I get by." He drained the rest of his coffee and handed the cup back to her. "That was most welcome. I'm touched by your kindness." It seemed a strange thing for him to say.

Hannah smiled at him. "You almost didn't get it. I had a bit of a disaster with one of my pans. Water everywhere."

"What happened?" His face was etched with concern.

"The handle fell off. It's been like that for ages. Same with a few of my other pans." She raised her eyebrows to indicate it was a real pain.

"You want me to *kumm* in and see if I can fix it?" Noah asked.

Hannah shook her head and felt redness in her cheeks. That wasn't why she had mentioned it. She was after all just trying to make conversation. "*Nee*, I couldn't ask that. Besides, I'm planning on getting a new set just after Christmas."

Noah nodded. "Right, I'd better get back to this fence. You'd better get back inside—it's cold out here."

"I thought you said you couldn't feel the cold?" she pointed out, a little confused. She could see the goosebumps on his arms.

"*Ach, jah*, I don't feel the cold when I'm working, that is. *Danke* again for the *kaffe*." He turned back to his fence post as if she wasn't even there.

Hannah stood watching him for a few more seconds before turning to walk back to the house. Suddenly, she stopped.

"Do *kumm* to the carol service tonight, Noah. It'll do you *gut*."

"I'll think about it," he replied gruffly. But Noah didn't meet her eyes. She watched as he drove the fence post in a few more inches, then turned and headed back inside the house.

CHAPTER 10

"See, I told you there would be donuts," Hannah said, squeezing Rachel's shoulder. "How many would you like?"

They stood in front of a red stand that smelt divine, with a line of people queued in front waiting for their tune to buy the sugary snack.

"I'll have ten," Aaron piped in.

"You'll be sick," Hannah objected.

Hannah was beginning to think they would arrive late to the caroling. Up until this point, Rachel had been very strong when it came to the loss of their father. She could barely remember their mother's death, being so young at the time. Other than a few nights of tears after he died, Rachel had hardly mentioned it at all. Children were, after all, so resilient.

But today was different. Shortly after lunch, when Hannah started talking about getting ready to go to the caroling, Rachel dug in her heels and said she wasn't going. She said it wouldn't be the same without their *daed* and that she wanted to stay home.

Then the tears started to flow. Everyone tried to comfort her, even Aaron.

But for an hour, there was no consoling her.

Finally, Aaron said something that actually hit home with her. "*Daed* would expect us to go. It's what he would want."

Hannah knew very well that her younger brother was correct. It was exactly what their father would have wanted.

Rachel heard those words, and suddenly the tears stopped.

After wiping her eyes, she agreed she should go. Hannah then sweetened the visit a little more by reminding everyone about the famous donut stand. Warm donuts were made in the square in the middle of town, with the proceeds going to charity.

It was Anna and her husband who ran the stand. She was pleased when Hannah went over and bought 16 doughnuts for the *familye* to share. They exchanged pleasantries, and once again, watching Anna take part in a charitable activity made Hannah wonder if she could be the Secret Santa.

Leah said she would have her donuts at home later because she had to help the bishop now.

Hannah edged through the crowds to ensure they got a good spot so Rachel could see. Aaron, by this point, had lost interest in the actual activities and was too busy licking his fingers of the remnants of his donuts, which he consumed as though someone might steal them right out of his hands.

They stood in a semicircle and watched as Bishop John King directed matters at the front. Leah rushed around at the bishop's direction, together with the other young Amish girls, handing candles out to the crowd.

Rachel munched on her donut as if all the upset from a few hours ago had never happened.

Hannah knew it would do her sister good to have a good cry and let her feelings out.

It was something she knew she would need to do at some point.

As they stood there, snippets of conversation flew around them.

Apparently, the Schrock family had received a box of new tools the night before, another gift from

Secret Santa. It was particularly welcome, considering the disaster that had befallen them earlier in the year.

Hannah was glad it wasn't just her family benefitting from Secret Santa's generosity.

Subconsciously she started scanning the crowd. Looking at faces. To start with, she didn't know why she was doing it. Then it came to her, and when it did, she flinched a little in shock, causing Rachel to look at her to check if anything was wrong.

Hannah knew she was looking for Noah.

But she had no idea why.

It brought with it both troubling and exciting thoughts.

She caught a glimpse of Gideon standing on the far side, in the front row of the semicircle. He seemed to catch Hannah's eye and smiled. It had a glint of mischief about it.

It brought her back to the present and away from her thoughts. She smiled back.

She wondered if that smile could've meant something. Was it his way of trying to acknowledge that he was behind the gifts they'd received?

Then she saw he was laughing and joking with the people next to him as well.

She was probably reading far too much into it.

Maybe she should just forget about who the Secret Santa was and get on with enjoying the festive season, making sure her siblings got through it without any further upsets like earlier that afternoon.

Then the bishop called everyone to order. His warm voice broke through the chat with an air of authority and power.

A hush fell over the crowd.

He gave a short talk about the importance of generosity and charity during this very special season.

Another thought came to Hannah that she hadn't really considered in much depth up to now. Could it be that Bishop John King himself was the Secret Santa? She cast her mind back. She couldn't really remember how long ago the gifts had started. Maybe it was around the time the bishop had been elected. She vaguely remembered the old bishop, an elderly man with a long beard that almost reached his stomach. When he passed, the suitable candidates' names were all put into a hat, and John's name was pulled out. Was that when the gifts started?

Hannah had been young at the time—probably even younger than Rachel was now.

Maybe she would ask someone before they went home.

Everyone clapped once the bishop finished speaking, and then the caroling started. During the first one, a light went around the group so they could all light the candles that had been passed around a few minutes before.

"Hold it carefully," Hannah whispered to Rachel in concern. She glanced over to Aaron and said nothing but gave him a look that suggested he should not do anything stupid with the flame.

They all sang by candlelight, and Hannah allowed the comfort of a silent tear to fall down her face as she remembered Christmases long past; ones she had enjoyed with both of her parents. Of course, nothing could ever be the same again, but that didn't mean there wasn't a future to look forward to.

And then she saw him.

Noah.

Moving around the back of the crowd on the far side. It was only now that he was amongst so many people, that she realized how tall Noah actually was.

He held no candle, but he was illuminated by those around him.

Noah turned his head slightly and looked at Hannah. Instantly, her stomach flipped as their eyes met. Her heart pounded in her chest. Her breath shallowed and she found herself unable to look away.

She had never had such a reaction to a man before.

And once more, she felt those conflicting, troubling, and exciting thoughts.

Her whole body seemed to tighten as she held his gaze. She smiled and forgot to keep singing.

Rachel turned her face upwards towards her, "Why are you gripping my shoulder so tightly?"

Hannah turned to look down at her sister. "Sorry, little one." She slackened her grip on her sister, who relaxed and turned back to the event.

Hannah looked back over to where Noah had been standing.

But he was gone.

CHAPTER 11

The caroling came to a close, but people were reluctant to leave for home. It was as if everyone enjoyed this sense of community.

Once more, Hannah found herself scanning the crowd, looking for Noah. If she saw him, she wanted to say hello, to ask if he had enjoyed the event. But she couldn't find him anywhere in the crowd.

Leah returned to the family group, pleased with her efforts in making the service a success, and was chattering away to Rachel and Aaron.

Then Hannah's eyes fell on Naomi Bender. She was saying goodbye to an elderly Amish couple before turning to walk in the direction of her home. Quickly, Hannah reached into her dress and pulled out some more money. She handed it to Leah.

"Why don't you take these two and go buy some more donuts for them? I'm just going to speak to Naomi quickly."

Aaron squealed in excitement, "I'm going to have ten." He repeated the same demand as earlier.

Hannah laughed and raised her finger. "*Nee,* you're not," she looked at her sister. "Be sensible, Leah."

Her sister smiled and nodded her head in understanding.

"Let's go! *Danke,* Hannah!" Aaron managed to shout as he dragged the two sisters through the crowd toward Anna's stand.

Hannah watched them for the briefest of moments, then quickly moved off and caught up with Naomi.

"Hello, Hannah. How are you? Where are your siblings?" Naomi asked, looking around.

"Leah's taking them to the donut stand. A special treat. I think they deserve it, with everything they've been through this year."

Naomi gave her a sympathetic smile and reached out to touch her shoulder. "You've done such an amazing job with them, Hannah."

Hannah smiled, "Don't. I've cried enough. But thank you for the kind words." She took a moment to blink back the tears that were already forming in her eyes, then took a step closer. "I have a question for you."

"I told you before, I'm not the Secret Santa," Naomi laughed.

Hannah shook her head. "*Nee*, it's not about that. It's about Noah Beiler."

Naomi tilted her head, a hint of suspicion in her eyes. "What about him?"

"What do you know about him?"

"Why do you want to know?" Naomi asked, her tone curious.

"It's just..." Hannah paused as she considered how to phrase this so it wouldn't sound strange. "He came over and fixed our fence earlier today. It had been knocked down in the snowstorm, and he just fixed it. It seemed a little odd, that's all. I realized I don't know much about him."

"That sounds like Noah," Naomi said. "He is a bit strange, I have to say. But I suppose he would be, considering his background."

Hannah was desperate to ask what she meant, but instead, she kept silent, letting the older woman continue.

"His *daed* left, you know that?"

Hannah shook her head.

"Well, let me tell you the story. When Noah was just five, his *daed* disappeared in the middle of the night to join the *Englisch*. Noah's poor mother, Sadie, was frantic. The community did what they could to help at the time, but no one ever heard from him again. Then, a petition came through in the mail; he wanted a divorce. Obviously, Sadie refused to sign it, but you know what these legal matters are. After a few years, it got pushed through the courts anyway, so Sadie had no choice."

Hannah, of course, had no idea how legal matters proceeded, especially when they involved the *Englisch* world.

"I didn't realize."

"Sadie always considered herself married. Despite what the courts said, she believed she was still Leroy Beiler's wife. She never looked for a new husband, she didn't think it was right. She went about raising Noah alone. She did an admirable job, considering the circumstances and what little she was left with, or rather, not left with, if you catch my meaning." Naomi shifted her feet for a second, collecting her thoughts. "Then, of course, Noah's mother died. He was only young. Well, not so young, maybe your Leah's age, give or take. Fifteen, isn't she?"

"Who looked after him?" Hannah asked after she had nodded to confirm her sister's age.

"No one. He refused to move out of the *haus*. He was fifteen, so of course, the community rallied around and offered what they could, but aside from accepting some food, he refused all support. The bishop tried to persuade him to move in with one of his aunts or uncles, but he said he'd rather leave the community. At fifteen, he almost looked like a *mann*. You can see how tall he is now, I guess he was almost that size then. Time passed, and before we knew it, he turned into a *mann* anyway, and that was that."

"What does he do for work?"

"I'm not sure he does work. His *haus* has enough land for him to grow plenty of food to support himself, I guess. I understand he does some woodwork, but whether he sells any of it, I don't know."

"How does he make ends meet, then?"

"His *mamm* did leave him some money, as I say she did a *gut* job of raising him. But a year or so after she died, he learned his father had also passed away in the city. Despite divorcing Sadie, his father had not remarried, and Noah inherited what his father had. From what I hear, and it's mostly rumors, you understand, it was a considerable sum."

"Such a tragedy on all levels, isn't it?" Hannah said softly.

"Very much like your own, Hannah. Even though Noah received money, it didn't make his loss any easier to bear. I miss his *mamm*. Sadie was *wunderbar*, very generous. She didn't let her situation get in the way of helping others. She did so much for the community. She was a wonder with medicines. She'd make her own out of herbs. Honestly, the number of illnesses she managed to cure over the years. People would form lines outside her place to get her to mix up something for them."

Hannah nodded, feeling sorry for Noah. She couldn't imagine being left without anyone in the world. Yes, she was still grieving her parents, but she still had her siblings—siblings she knew she had a responsibility to care for.

She couldn't imagine them fending for themselves in the big, wide world like Noah had. Maybe that explained why he was the way he was.

"How old is he, actually?" She thought back to Noah, swinging the hammer with effortless ease, the flecks of gray mingling with the snow in his hair.

Naomi thought for a moment, then shrugged. "Late twenties, I'd guess."

"And he's never married?"

"Obviously not. I'm not involved much with town gossip, but I don't believe he's ever courted. I don't know why. He's a *gut*-looking *mann*, actually, in his own strange way."

Hannah didn't respond, she seemed lost in thought.

Naomi studied Hannah closely and then smiled knowingly, she took a step forward and whispered in her ear, "My own husband was over ten years older than me. It worked out perfectly, you know."

CHAPTER 12

The crowd finally began to disperse, and the Fisher familye started making their way home.

"Did you enjoy that, Rachel?" Hannah asked as they walked.

"*Jah*. There's something about the carol singing that feels almost magical," the little girl said with a yawn, reaching up to hold Hannah's hand.

"Are you tired?" Hannah asked softly.

"A little," Rachel replied.

"What, after all that sugar?" Leah laughed. "You'll be awake for days."

Aaron was walking a few paces behind them, still munching on the remnants of his donuts.

"He will," Hannah chuckled, nodding in her

brother's direction. "At least nobody has to get up for school in the morning."

"Look!" Aaron suddenly shouted, pointing up toward the heavens.

"Oh, my," Hannah exclaimed.

A shooting star streaked across the darkness in front of them, bathing the sky in yellow, orange, and blue for just a brief moment.

"What was that?" Rachel asked. "It was beautiful."

"A shooting star. I think it's a sign sent especially for us at Christmas," Hannah said.

"Do you think *Daed* sent it?" Rachel asked softly.

Hannah glanced at Leah and saw her turn away. She suspected Rachel's words had brought a tear to her sister's eye. But she didn't press the girl. Instead, she stopped walking and crouched down to Rachel's level.

"*Jah*, I do. I think it's *Daed's* way of telling us he's all right and happy now that he's reunited with *Mamm* in heaven."

Rachel smiled in the innocent way only children can. "I'm glad. It is Christmas, after all. He deserves to be happy."

It took all of Hannah's effort not to break down in front of everyone. She swallowed back her emotions and stood up.

The family walked on in silence until they reached home, each alone with their own thoughts.

Having moved from the back to the front, Aaron asked, "Can we have a snack before bed?"

"A snack? You've eaten enough to feed a horse," Hannah teased.

"I'm hungry," Aaron complained, rubbing his stomach.

"Maybe I could make some ham sandwiches if everyone would like that?"

There was a chorus of approval. Leah's tears had dried up, and she was now walking along quite happily.

Then there was a sudden squeal of excitement from Aaron at the front. "There's another gift!"

He stopped in his tracks, pointed at the gift, and turned to look at his three sisters following behind.

The three girls all glanced at each other, and in an instant, all three of them sprang forward, shouting and screaming in delight at the sight of the largest parcel yet. Hannah for once, behaving like the other two, charging ahead in an effort to get there first.

Once again, it was wrapped neatly in brown paper and tied with a red ribbon.

All four just stood and looked in wonder at the huge gift on the porch.

"Secret Santa strikes again, but this rules out the bishop, doesn't it?" Hannah said, looking in Leah's direction. "He was there the entire night at the caroling."

"But did you see his wife?" Leah asked.

Hannah thought for a moment, then shook her head. She hadn't seen Katie at all. "Not that I recall, but there were so many people there."

"Maybe it's all part of his plan to cover his tracks. Maybe it is the bishop, and he just sent Katie out to deliver tonight," Leah said.

"I didn't see her either," Aaron said in agreement.

Hannah smiled, that really didn't mean much. If Aaron couldn't eat it or play with it, then it would be likely that he hadn't seen it.

"I don't care, I want to see what's inside!" Rachel said, jumping up and down in excitement. Any sign of tiredness had now evaporated.

They tried to lift the parcel, but it was far too heavy. In the end, they resorted to dragging it inside. Hannah and Leah ended up pulling, with Aaron and Rachel at the front pushing with all their strength.

A huge wedge of snow built up in front of it as it went. Once they finally pushed it inside the house, they stopped to kick the snow away. After ten minutes of effort, it was inside the kitchen, and all four were breathing heavily from the exertion.

"Hannah, please open it," Rachel demanded once they had got their breath back.

Hannah obliged and opened the box, only to take two steps back in shock.

Inside was a whole new set of cookware, and all manner of kitchenware.

Hannah and Leah stared down at the contents. Rachel showed some interest but didn't find it particularly exciting.

"I would've preferred some saws and hammers like the Schrocks got," Aaron said after examining one skillet.

"But these are exactly what we need, Aaron. I spilled water all over myself today while making *kaffe* for Noah," Hannah said.

Then she froze, holding up the stockpot she had just removed from the box.

Noah.

How could the Secret Santa have known they needed a new set of cookware? Was it just a coincidence? After all, the winter clothing they needed must have been a coincidence. But today, she'd told

Noah she was planning to buy a new set of cookware after Christmas.

"What is it?" Leah asked, looking at Hannah, confused.

Hannah didn't answer right away. After a long pause, she said, "Nothing. I'm just amazed that it's exactly what we needed. We've been so blessed by these gifts."

"We're the luckiest *familye* in the community!" Rachel declared with all the authority of a child.

Hannah and Leah, of course, knew they weren't. The only reason they were receiving the gifts was because they hadn't been so lucky this year. But they weren't about to explain that and spoil the wonder of it all for Rachel. Instead, Hannah ruffled her sister's hair.

"I think we are."

It took Hannah and Leah a full ten minutes to unpack the box. Once again, they were astounded by the array of goods. There were pots, pans, skillets, roasting pans, baking sheets, and casserole dishes. But the parcel didn't just stop at cookware, there were spatulas, ladles, cutting boards, mixing bowls, whisks, and graters as well. And bakeware from muffin tins to pie dishes. Then, finally, at the bottom, a new knife block, with five brand-new high-quality knives.

"Who could've bought all this? It must've cost hundreds," Leah whispered to Hannah.

"More than that. Thousands, probably," Hannah replied, trying to add the cost in her mind but failing.

Once again, Hannah's thoughts drifted to Noah.

She had seen him at the caroling that night. It wasn't a figment of her imagination. He had definitely been there, and he had definitely seen her. Could it be that he'd slipped away early and perhaps delivered this parcel?

She remembered the strange encounter with him a few days ago, on the very day the first Secret Santa gift arrived. He'd shouted at the children for throwing snowballs. He was heading away from their house.

She glanced out of the window into the darkness but in the direction of the fence he had repaired earlier that day. She almost saw him swinging that huge hammer with effortless ease.

He was strong enough to lift these gifts by himself.

Slowly the pieces were starting to fit.

Then she remembered the words of Naomi

Bender, and how Noah's mother had been known for her generosity.

Could it be that she had solved the mystery of the Amish Secret Santa?

Could it be that it was a man that almost no one would suspect?

CHAPTER 13

The next morning, Hannah rose from bed, tired and with her head aching. Her sleep had been fitful and disturbed. She kept asking herself who could be sending the mystery gifts, over and over in her mind. She wrestled with the question of who the Secret Santa might be. Last night, she had believed she was closer than ever to confirming an identity. But still, doubts lingered and those intensified the more she tossed and turned in bed.

Maybe her suspicions that the bishop and his family were behind the gifts were more likely. After all, how would Noah Beiler, a man who kept himself isolated from much of the community, know about the struggles and tribulations that various families had been going through throughout the year? This was a man who didn't seem capable of buying himself a winter coat. How could he buy a whole range of suitable gifts for others?

Something else had been weighing on her mind that night; Noah Beiler himself.

The way her body had reacted when she saw him at the caroling last night. That strange feeling in the pit of her stomach, the quickening of her pulse. This wasn't something that should have been happening to her. Not now, not with the responsibilities she had. She had her siblings to look after, acting as their mother. Any thoughts of Noah Beiler in that way needed to be pushed aside.

Finally, her siblings began to emerge from the bedroom one by one. Leah first, followed by Rachel. Hannah put thoughts of her throbbing head to one side and began to make breakfast.

Eggs and bacon were on the menu this morning. It was, after all, close to Christmas.

She called for Aaron just as she was about to start serving. There was no sign of the boy. She called again but to no avail.

"Leah, wake Aaron, please."

Leah nodded, stood up, and disappeared from the kitchen. Hannah slid the first plate of bacon and eggs in front of Rachel, who began to tuck in heartily. It seemed that yesterday's upset had been forgotten. For that, Hannah was thankful. She knew perfectly well that their father wouldn't want Rachel to be upset.

"Hannah, Hannah!" came Leah's sudden shout, filled with panic.

Immediately, Hannah's stomach dropped, and nervous tension gripped her entire body. This wasn't the kind of shout that brought good news. She almost dropped Aaron's breakfast plate back on the counter and rushed to his bedroom.

Leah was bent over him, feeling the boy's forehead. At once, Hannah could see that Aaron was burning up with a fever. Sweat covered his face.

"He's hot," Leah said, her voice soft. "Very hot."

Hannah rushed to her brother's side. "Aaron, talk to me, it's Hannah," she urged.

The boy opened his eyes and smiled weakly. "Hello, Hannah. I'm a bit hot. I don't think I'm feeling well. But I don't think it was the donuts," he said with a small grin.

Despite her worry, Hannah couldn't help but smile back at the boy's joke. At least he hadn't lost his sense of humor. "You'll be all right. We just need to try to break your fever."

Ten minutes later, Aaron was lying in bed with a cold towel on his forehead, and the bedcovers removed. The window was open, bringing in a cold breeze.

An hour later, things hadn't improved. If anything, they seemed to be getting worse. Aaron was still talking and cracking jokes, though. At one point, he even asked for more donuts. This gave Hannah and Leah some degree of comfort. Rachel had been given Aaron's plate of breakfast as well and was told to go and play with her faceless dolls.

"I'm going into town to get some medicine," Hannah finally said to Leah. "Keep him cool and keep replacing the towel until I'm back."

"What's happening?" Rachel asked as Hannah pulled on her coat in the hallway.

"I'm just going into town to get some medicine for your *Bruder*. You'll be a *gut* girl for Leah, all right? Do you understand?" Hannah asked, trying to keep her voice calm.

"Will Aaron be all right? Is he going to die?" concern was etched on Rachel's young face.

Immediately, Hannah crouched down and gently grasped Rachel's shoulders. She shook her head.

"He's just got a fever, that's all. Aaron's not going to die. I promise."

She wanted to stay and reassure Rachel a little longer, but there was no time. With Christmas approaching, she was unsure of the store hours in town. She needed to get there and back quickly to ensure Aaron received the medicine he needed.

She stepped out into the snow. Another flurry had fallen overnight, and the ground was thickly blanketed in white.

She was nearly in town when she spotted a figure walking toward her with a small grocery bag tucked under his arm. It was Noah.

"*Gut* day to you, Hannah. How are you?" he asked with surprising joviality in his tone.

"I'm all right, *danke*, Noah. I think I saw you at the caroling last night. Did you enjoy it?"

"*Ach, jah*, I was there. I saw you too, remember?" Noah replied.

For the first time in hours, her thoughts returned to that strange feeling in her stomach when she'd seen him.

"I remember," she paused for a second, once again wondering how on earth he could stand being out in the cold in just his shirtsleeves. "I'd love to stop and chat, but I can't. I'm rushing into town. Aaron is sick with a fever, and I need to get him some medicine."

Noah nodded. "A fever? The poor boy," he spoke

in broken sentences as if trying to think of something. "*Jah*, I understand. You must go."

Hannah smiled at him and nodded her head before hurrying into town without saying another word. Noah would have to wait; she had a duty to her brother.

Two hours later, she was pacing Aaron's bedroom. She had managed to purchase some medicine, and Aaron had taken it willingly. Now, she was just waiting for the fever to break. But so far, there had been no progress. Every time she touched his forehead, it felt as though it was on fire.

There was an unexpected knock at the front door. "Leah, can you get that?" Hannah called out.

She heard the door open and felt an icy gust of wind rush inside, followed by some quiet conversation between Leah and whoever was at the door. Then came the sound of heavy footsteps in the hallway. Hannah turned to open Aaron's bedroom door and was surprised to see Noah standing in the hallway at Leah's side.

"It's Noah, Hannah," Leah said. "He says he's got something that might help Aaron."

She looked a little unsure about whether she should have let Noah inside.

Noah opened his hand to show a small bottle of

green liquid in the palm of his hand. Hannah stared at it, confused.

"It's one of my *mamm's* concoctions. I made it up after we spoke today. This will break a fever within the hour," he said, the pride evident in his voice. He took the vial between his thumb and forefinger and shook it slightly.

Both Hannah and Leah exchanged skeptical glances, and then Hannah looked at the strange green liquid. She remembered what Naomi had said the night before: *"She was a wonder with medicines. She'd make her own out of herbs. Honestly the number of illnesses she managed to cure over the years. People would form lines outside her place to get her to mix up something for them."*

"I promise I won't do anything to hurt him further," Noah said, seeing Hannah's hesitation. "My *mamm* was an absolute wonder with medicines."

"I know," Hannah replied. "Okay, *danke*. We'll try it," she said, stepping forward and taking the green liquid from Noah.

"One spoonful; that's all it should take," Noah said.

"The fever should break within an hour?" Hannah asked.

Noah nodded. "Always does."

There was such conviction in his voice that Hannah believed him; any doubts in her mind were washed away.

Just then, Rachel appeared from the direction of the bathroom. "Hannah, there's a problem in there. It's not flushing."

Hannah sighed. "Just what we need before Christmas."

"Would you like me to take a look at it? I'm quite *gut* with plumbing," Noah offered cheerfully.

"*Ach, nee*, you've done so much for us already. I couldn't possibly ask," Hannah began,

"Honestly, it's no problem. I'm here, after all. I'm guessing none of you have any plumbing skills?" Noah placed his hat on the chair in the hallway, as though the decision had been made and he was staying.

Hannah conceded that they didn't. Having to use the old outhouse that was still standing outside by the barn was not an appealing prospect over Christmas, especially in this weather.

"If you don't mind Noah, I would truly appreciate it."

"Do you have any tools?" Noah asked, clasping his hands together as though eager to do the work.

"We've still got all of *Daed's* out in the barn," Hannah said.

Noah nodded. "You go give that to the young one, and I'll go see what tools we've got and check out the problem."

Hannah nodded her agreement, and Noah disappeared toward the barn. The Fischers called it a barn but in reality, it was more of a shed. The family weren't farmers, so there was no need for a large barn; it served its purpose for storage and such.

Father had planned to do some repairs on it before his death. It was just one thing on a long list of jobs that needed doing around the property, but those would be concerns for spring. Right now, she had to see to her brother.

CHAPTER 14

The next hour was filled with a series of bangs and crashes emerging from the bathroom at the Fisher house.

"Do you really think he knows what he's doing in there?" asked Leah

"We can only hope so," Hannah replied.

Finally, the door opened, and Noah wore a triumphant smile on his face. "It's fixed. You shouldn't have any more problems now."

Rachel clapped her hands together as if it was the most magnificent thing she'd ever heard.

"My window hasn't opened since summer. It gets so hot in there. Can you fix that as well?"

"Rachel," Hannah scolded. "That's rude. You don't

ask questions like that. I'm sorry, Noah, she shouldn't have…"

"No trouble at all." Noah interrupted. "Why don't you *kumm* and show me, little one? Let me see what I can do."

Rachel reached up to grab Noah's hand and pulled him into her bedroom. Leah turned to Hannah and laughed, and her older sister couldn't help but offer her a smile in return.

Suddenly, Hannah and Leah heard the patter of footsteps behind them. They turned to see Aaron in his nightshirt, out of bed. He yawned as though he had just woken from a normal night's sleep.

"Did I miss breakfast? I smell bacon!"

Hannah glanced at the clock over the fireplace. It had been 57 minutes since she had administered Noah's green magical liquid. The fever had broken; Noah's mother's concoction had cured Aaron. It was a Christmas miracle! She closed her eyes for a brief second.

A few hours later, Noah was still at the Fisher residence. He had managed to fix Rachel's window. She might not want it open right now due to the cold temperatures, but Hannah was glad as it would stop her younger sister from moaning during the height of next summer. Noah was now in the barn, saying he had noticed some small holes in the back when he was searching for the appropriate tools to fix the plumbing.

"Rats will be in if you're not careful," he declared in a firm voice. "I'll need to fix those before I go home."

Despite her personal shame that he felt compelled to have to complete all these jobs around the place, Hannah had seen enough of him by now not to argue. She knew the man liked to be helpful.

Hannah cooked Aaron some more bacon and eggs, only too pleased to see him now back to health. It was strange, considering the state he'd been in just a few hours ago, to see him wolfing down his food and then asking if there was any more.

Now he was reading a book in the living room while Rachel played with her dolls on the floor. It was as if he had no idea of the worry he had caused.

Hannah and Leah were deep in conversation at the kitchen table, sipping coffee.

"Do you think they'll mind? It is Christmas Eve, after all. And it is a time for *familye*," Hannah asked, tilting her head towards Aaron and Rachel in the living room.

"I don't think so. He seemed to get on very well with Rachel, didn't he? She was chattering away to him while he fixed her window, as though he were…" Leah paused as if she didn't want to say the words out loud, as if it would be disrespectful in some way.

But Hannah knew perfectly well what her sister was going to say and finished the sentence for her. "As though he were *Daed*."

Leah nodded and gave a sad smile, "I have not seen her so animated in conversation over the last few months."

Hannah gave a soft laugh. "That can only be a *gut* thing. And I doubt Aaron is going to mind, as long as he gets fed."

"I think it's a *gut* suggestion of yours. It's only right, considering everything he's done," Leah said.

"All right, I'll go and ask him. Let me take him some more *kaffe* and one of your cinnamon rolls. He devoured one the other day, you know."

Two minutes later, she was heading out toward the barn, a cup of coffee in hand and a wrapped cinnamon roll tucked in her coat pocket.

The sounds of hammering came from the barn. She walked inside, and for a second she couldn't see him.

"Noah?" she called.

He emerged from the darkness at the rear. "I

105

found a few more bits that needed repairing. A bit of rot, I'm afraid. If I left it over winter, I doubt this place would still be standing by this time next year. I've done the worst of it. I'll be back to finish when the weather is a bit more favorable."

"Thank you for everything you've done, Noah," Hannah said, handing him the coffee and cinnamon roll.

"*Danke*," he replied, looking at the cinnamon roll with appreciation.

"There's something else as well. We'd like to invite you to dinner tomorrow evening. If you're willing, that is."

"It's Christmas Eve?" Noah said, surprised.

"I know. But do you have somewhere else to go on Christmas Eve?" Hannah asked.

Noah looked thoughtful and shook his head. "*Nee*. Not at all. Everything is done by then."

"What do you mean by everything is done?" she asked.

He looked slightly taken aback as if he'd said something he hadn't meant to. "Oh, it's just that Christmas Eve is normally a time for families. Don't you all want to be together, especially considering… well, the year you've had?"

"We are all together. We've discussed it as a

familye and we would love for you to join us, Noah. Especially me."

No sooner had the final words left her lips than she wished she could take them back. She hadn't planned to say it out loud. It was meant to be a thought in her head, reserved for her alone. Her cheeks went bright red with embarrassment.

Noah smiled softly. "I'd like that very much, Hannah. *Danke.* I appreciate it."

They stood staring at each other for a few moments. Once again, she felt that strange sensation in her stomach. And again, the words of Naomi Bender came to her: *"My own husband was over ten years older than me. It worked out perfectly, you know."*

She thought of Noah and how Rachel had laughed and chattered while he fixed the window. He had almost turned into a different person since that encounter in the snow a few days ago. Noah could easily become a father figure to her younger siblings. Naomi's husband had been older than her. Many Amish women's husbands were older. It worked for them. Could it work for her, she wondered.

"Your mother must have been a remarkable woman," she said, finally breaking the strange silence between them.

He took a sip of his coffee and smiled. "That she was. You wouldn't know the half of it, Hannah. The way she managed after my father left the community, raising me on her own. She'd have liked you. I know that much. What you've done for your siblings, given the circumstances, is nothing short of remarkable."

"It must've been terrible for you, your father disappearing like that," Hannah said brushing past the compliment in case it caused her to become emotional again.

Noah went pale for a moment, lowering his coffee cup.

Hannah immediately knew she'd touched a sensitive subject. "I'm sorry if I spoke out of turn. It's none of my business, of course."

"*Nee*, I'm happy to share. *Jah*, I suppose in some ways, I wish he'd died," Noah said. "I know that sounds terrible and harsh, an awful thing for a *sohn* to say. But it was as if he'd rejected me. I was there, a *kind* needing care, and he chose to go somewhere else. That kind of pain never left me, and it made me realize that I never wanted to be hurt like that again."

"That's terrible," Hannah said, sitting on a bale of hay that was set aside for feeding the horse over the next month or so. She patted the space beside her, encouraging him to sit down. He responded without question.

"I guess that's why I am the way I am. I know I live a bit differently, but I never wanted to integrate, just in case I got hurt again. It's my way of coping, I guess. That is, until recently..."

"What do you mean?" Hannah asked, once again feeling butterflies in her stomach.

"Oh, just that over recent months, I've realized I don't want to live the rest of my life alone. I'd like what everyone else in the community has: a *familye*, maybe even some friends. But, at my age, well, it's difficult."

"At your age? How old are you?" Hannah asked.

"Twenty-eight," he said, looking a little self-conscious.

"Twenty-eight? That's nothing. There are plenty of Amish women with older husbands," Hannah said.

Once again, she felt the color rise to her face and wondered if she'd spoken out of turn. It almost felt as if she was hinting that she could be his wife. She suddenly realized that maybe she was. Somehow, the words had escaped her lips because that's what she truly wanted.

He smiled at her, "Well, we'll see what the future

brings. That's all any of us can do. So, for dinner tomorrow, what time should I *kumm*?"

"Let's say five in the evening. We can play some board games afterward if you like that sort of thing. Rachel adores board games, and so does Aaron, although you have to watch him; he'll cheat if you're not careful."

Noah laughed. "All young *menner* are the same, I'm sure. I'm glad he's back on his feet."

"All thanks to your *mamm's* concoction."

"I told you it would work," Noah said.

"You did."

"I'll take the cinnamon roll home if I may. I'll have it tonight before bed," he said. "I've got some things to do over the other side of town, so I'd better be off."

"Really, at this time of day? It's getting dark," Hannah said.

"*Jah*, I have a delivery to make," Noah replied, slightly hesitant.

"Oh, do you?" Hannah said, giving him a sideways look. For a moment, they locked eyes. Hannah saw secrets in those eyes, secrets that he wasn't yet ready to share.

He nodded quickly. "Right, I'd better go."

They walked together from the barn toward the

house. "It's freezing out here tonight. Look at you—still in your shirtsleeves! You'll make yourself ill," she chided.

"Well, I don't get out much. No need for a coat, normally. As I said, when I'm working, I don't feel the cold."

Hannah shook her head, still shocked that the man didn't have a coat. Then she remembered something. Her father's coat, which was far too big for Aaron and would be for many years, was wasted where it was.

"Wait here."

She ran inside and rummaged through one of the old wardrobes. A few minutes later, she emerged holding a black coat.

"This was my *daed's*."

Noah's eyes grew wide. "It's perfect, Hannah. I'll take *gut* care of it and bring it back tomorrow."

"You don't have to bring it back. It's yours now," she said, handing it to him with a grateful smile.

"Mine?" He pulled it on, almost in disbelief.

She stepped forward and gently took his hand. "*Danke*, Noah…" she paused and then looked him in the eye once again. "For everything. I think you know what I mean."

Noah looked back and just nodded his head.

CHAPTER 15

"**S**top," Leah demanded with a laugh, grabbing her sister by the shoulders. "No need to be so nervous."

Hannah looked back at Leah. Sometimes, when Leah wasn't full of teenage impulses, she acted as though she was the older sister.

"Does it show that much?"

"You've been checking that the kitchen table is set correctly for the past 20 minutes. You've cleaned the living room twice, and the floor is so shiny, I'm sure I can see my face in it."

"Oh, I see," Hannah replied. "It's just a dinner to say thank you," she added, noticing Leah's skeptical gaze.

"If you say so," Leah responded slowly, making it clear she didn't believe a single word.

A deliberate knock on the door came at exactly five minutes before five. "Early. He's keen," Leah teased, jabbing Hannah in the ribs.

Hannah laughed and playfully punched her sister in the arm. "None of that, especially not while he's here and definitely not in front of the other two."

Leah threw her hands up, feigning innocence. "I have no idea what you're talking about."

"*Jah*, you do."

"Answer the door, Hannah. We can't leave the *mann* standing outside."

Hannah took a deep breath, smoothed down her dress, and went to the door. When she opened it, Noah stood to the side, wearing her father's coat, and with his hat in his hand. On the top of the step was a large parcel wrapped in the now customary brown paper and red string.

"It looks like you had a delivery before I arrived," Noah said, nervously glancing down at the package.

Hannah eyed him with suspicion. By now, she was almost certain that Noah was the Secret Santa. All the pieces were in place. They'd been home all day without hearing anyone arrive or seeing anyone walk down the drive. It was the better part of an hour into dusk, so it was possible someone could have sneaked down the drive under cover of darkness. But wouldn't it make more sense if Noah had brought it in his own buggy, now parked just a few yards away and he had placed it there before he knocked?

But she couldn't fault him; he was playing his part to perfection.

For now, she decided to let it go. "This is rather exciting, isn't it? *Gut* evening, by the way, Noah. Glad you could make it."

"Thank you for inviting me."

"No problem. Just a little way of saying thank you, that's all. You've done so much for us over the last few weeks."

Noah looked a bit embarrassed by the compliment. "Do you want me to help bring this inside?"

"Aaron, Rachel, Leah we've got another gift from Secret Santa!" Hannah called, directing her words indoors.

The younger kids came running, full of excitement. Leah joined them after a few more seconds.

"How long has it been sitting out there?" Leah asked no one in particular.

"I don't know, it was here when I arrived," Noah said calmly.

"Take Noah and show him where to stable his horse. Leah and I will bring this inside," Hannah told Aaron, who started to object. "Don't worry, we won't open it until you're back."

Aaron nodded. "All right. *Kumm* on, Noah, let's get your horse settled, and then we can open the parcel and eat. I'm starving, are you?"

He ran off toward the buggy and after a moment, Noah followed. Hannah watched for a second, thrilled that the younger children seemed to take to Noah so easily.

Ten minutes later, Aaron brought him back in, with the horse safely stabled and enjoying a snack of hay.

"Let me take your coat, Noah," Hannah said.

Noah removed it and handed it to her. She hung it up on the same hook her father used to use. It had been months since his coat had hung there. She glanced at it, feeling a wave of sadness wash over her. She wished he and their mother were here to enjoy the festivities. But they couldn't be. She could only hope they were watching over them.

"Can I get you a drink?" Hannah offered.

"Water will be fine, *danke*," Noah replied.

As if on cue, Rachel ran to the kitchen and

returned with a glass of ice-cold water. "Here you go," she said, handing it to him.

"*Danke*, little one. Have you had that window open today?"

"It's too cold for that, silly," Rachel laughed.

Hannah gave her a sharp look; she knew very well that Noah was joking, but calling a visitor to the house "silly" felt a bit much.

"Well, shall we open this gift?" Leah interrupted.

"*Jah!*" Rachel exclaimed, clapping her hands in her usual excited way.

Very carefully, Hannah opened the box, once more taking care not to rip the brown paper. After this Christmas, they would have enough to last them years.

Inside were four individual gifts, each neatly labeled with white cards inscribed with beautiful calligraphy.

She pulled out a blue scented candle with Leah's name on it.

"This smells absolutely wonderful," Leah said, thrilled. "I'll keep this in my bedroom."

Next, she lifted out a volleyball labeled with Aaron's name. He took it, grinning.

"Wow, this is amazing!" He'd been joining in the community sporting events this year, and volleyball was his favorite. Now he had his own ball to practice with outside.

Then, Rachel opened her gift, it was a mysterious-looking box. She lifted the lid and gasped at the array of art supplies inside. "I'm going to paint a picture of the *haus* after dinner," she bubbled.

Finally, there was a gift for Hannah: a beautifully carved wooden heart, intricately engraved with a spattering of smaller hearts. It was a stunning piece that must've taken hours to create.

"It's beautiful," she cooed softly, running her fingers along its grooves.

She looked at Noah and smiled. He couldn't help but smile back and, once more, she felt that familiar flutter in her stomach as she met his steady gaze.

"Is it time to eat, then?" Aaron demanded, breaking the stare between Hannah and Noah.

"*Jah*, I guess it is. Secret Santa has been very kind to us, I have to say," Hannah said, more for Noah's benefit than anything.

They all moved into the kitchen. Hannah had been meticulous with the meal preparation tonight. She'd cooked the roast beef from the very first Secret Santa parcel as well as roasted potatoes, carrots, and red cabbage, followed by a large apple pie for dessert, with custard.

For once, Aaron had some competition at the dinner table when it came to eating. Noah heartily praised everything, savoring each bite.

Not for the first time in recent days, Hannah wondered how Noah managed day to day. What sort of meals did the man eat? How did he cope with laundry? Such things were not the work of men. She was amazed at how he managed every single day.

Afterward, they all helped clear the table, and the board games came out. Noah was a little rusty but soon got into the swing of things, rolling the dice and grinning in delight whenever he won.

Finally, it was the end of the evening, and Noah knew it was time to head home.

Hannah helped him with his coat in the hallway while Leah put Rachel to bed.

"*Danke* for tonight. It's been truly *wunderbar*."

"My pleasure, Noah," Hannah said, "I hope we can do it again sometime."

"I'll call on you after Christmas, if I may?"

"Absolutely. We'll probably have some more jobs that need doing by then," she said, grinning to let him know she was joking. She took a step closer to him and dropped her voice slightly, "The carved heart was something special."

"*Jah*, I'm sure Secret Santa put a lot of thought into it," Noah said.

"*Jah*, I'm sure he did, and I truly appreciate it," Hannah replied, opening the door. If Noah wanted to keep his secrets, she could wait.

She opened the door and gasped at the sight. Snow had fallen heavily, piling up almost four feet, and it was coming down so thick and fast that she couldn't even see the stables.

"You can't go home now. Not in this. It looks like I'll have to stay here for the night. We've got blankets and pillows; you can sleep on the living room floor."

Noah shook his head. "Really, it's fine. I couldn't possibly impose. Christmas morning is tomorrow; you should be with *familye*. I'll be fine."

Aaron came to the door, eyes wide. "Wow, I've never seen anything like it!"

"Noah isn't going anywhere, it's too dangerous," Hannah said firmly. "Aaron, get the bedding from the cupboard and make up the sofa."

"It'll be like an adventure. You'll love it, Noah. " Aaron said excitedly.

Noah took one last look at the snow and then stepped back inside. "Well, if you're sure?"

CHAPTER 16

$\mathcal{M}$ inutes after the stroke of midnight, Hannah decided she needed a glass of water.

She glanced at her clock and realized it was Christmas Day. She peeped out of the window and saw that the snow had slowed from the frenzy of earlier, but it was still coming down.

She pulled on her thick, long robe and opened her bedroom door. She crept out, taking care not to wake anyone.

Hannah was surprised to see the flicker of a candle in the living room. Surely Noah would be asleep? Had he forgotten to put out the candle?

Hannah was surprised to see him sitting in the rocking chair, reading their family bible. The pile of blankets and pillows was still neatly stacked on the sofa.

"What are you still doing awake, Noah?" Hannah asked softly.

He looked up, almost surprised to see her standing there. He shrugged his shoulders. "I always read a few pages of the Bible before I go to sleep. I guess I must've lost track of time. I was reading the openings of both Matthew and Luke."

"The Nativity. The birth of Jesus," Hannah said in a knowing way.

"Appropriate for the day I thought," Noah replied.

"Would you like a hot chocolate?" Hannah asked, now almost fully awake.

"That would be nice," Noah replied. "I can't remember the last time I had one."

"It's cold in here. Put another log on the fire," she ordered before leaving the room.

While she stood in the kitchen making hot chocolate, she could hardly believe that she was about to enjoy drinking it with a man in the early hours of Christmas morning. Such a thought would have been preposterous just a few weeks ago. Now, so much had changed, and yet so much remained unspoken between her and Noah. She tightened her robe, briefly wondering if she was perhaps unsuitably dressed. However, the robe reached her ankles and came high on her neck, and if anything, the sleeves were a little too long. She was probably more modestly dressed now than when she was fully clothed during the day.

She took the hot chocolate back to the living room. Noah had brought the fire back to life, and already it was warming the room. She handed him his hot chocolate and adjusted the gifts she had set out before she went to bed after her siblings had gone to sleep. She didn't want any accidents with the fire.

"It's very kind of you to let me stay. I truly don't want to intrude. I'll be gone first thing after dawn," Noah said.

Hannah shook her head. "You won't. The snow's still falling now. You'll stay. I insist."

He sipped his hot chocolate. "*Danke*, Hannah. I have to say, I like being here. Your *familye* is delightful. Little Rachel, she's a bundle of energy, isn't she? I do wish that I'd had a *schweschder*."

Hannah wondered for a moment what it might be like not to have any family whatsoever. She was still reeling from the loss of her parents, but at least she had her three siblings to cling to and nurture.

"And we like having you around."

"You know, it's strange, Hannah. As I mentioned to you yesterday, in recent months, I've started to realize that I want more from life than what I've been experiencing. I want a *familye* of my own. These past few days, spending time here with your *familye*," he paused, looking directly at Hannah, "and more specifically, with you, makes me wonder about what could be." He then offered a small laugh. "Of course, I'm being foolish. You're eighteen, I'm ten years older. You wouldn't be interested in a *mann* like me, with all my strange ways and habits." He glanced down at the floor.

"I'll be nineteen in a matter of weeks. And I have to say, since my *mamm* died three years ago, I rather feel I've matured very quickly. Even more so since *Daed* passed. I have the responsibilities of a much older person, do I not? I do not see age as a barrier. In fact, I see us well suited in that. Would an eighteen-year-old boy have the experiences of the world that I do?"

"So, you're saying there may well be a chance?"

Hannah felt more of those strange feelings in her stomach. She wondered if this was what love felt like. It seemed such a strange thing to define and understand. The love for a parent was one thing, but the love a woman might feel for a husband was different. She couldn't deny the flicker of excitement when Noah held her gaze. His eyes held a certain magical quality, they showed a deep kindness. The way he'd interacted with Rachel yesterday was heartwarming to see. For a man who hadn't had much interaction with others, he surely showed he had a good soul and a kind heart. He seemed ready to accept her siblings as part of her.

"There's always a chance, now, isn't there? Christmas is the time when miracles happen, isn't it?"

"When the snow clears, would you do me the honor of accompanying me on a buggy ride?" Noah asked after a moment's silence.

Hannah paused for a moment. This was the way courting was done in the Amish world; slowly and cautiously, and rightly so.

"On one condition."

"Name it," Noah replied. "And I understand that your *schweschdern* and *bruder* will always be your responsibility. I would consider them my responsibility as well."

In an instant, Noah had proved to her that her earlier thoughts were true. He would accept her siblings as part of her. She smiled at him and suddenly felt a wave of joy and happiness in her heart. It was a happiness that she hadn't felt in many months.

"*Nee*, it's not that, but I appreciate it with all my heart." She sat forward on the sofa. "*Kumm* on, tell me about Secret Santa. I swear on my life that I'll take the secret to my grave with me. I know it's you, there could be no one else."

Noah smiled back.

"It was something my *mamm* started many years ago. It was just small gifts left for a *familye* that seemed to have one tragedy after another over the course of one particular year. My mother wanted to help them out, but she knew they were proud people who wouldn't accept gifts if they knew where they came from. So she just left the gifts anonymously on their doorstep. It developed year after year. I knew about it, of course, I helped her deliver them as I grew older. When she died, it just seemed natural to me that honoring her memory meant continuing her tradition. It kept her close to my heart somehow."

It was such a beautiful thing for Noah to say.

"You know what?" Hannah replied. "People have told me that my parents would be very proud of me for everything I've done. But I know for certain that your mother would've been proud of you."

"I hope so." He bit his bottom lip as though trying

to hold back tears. "I hope that one day I can pass down the tradition to my own *kinner*."

Hannah thought about that for a second. She already had children, her siblings. But someday she wanted children of her own. What better man to have them with than a man with a heart as big as that of Noah Beiler?

EPILOGUE

*C*hristmas Eve, 2 Years Later

"Are you sure they're out?" Hannah asked, staring at the house in the darkness. It was the Millers' farmhouse, and this was their third visit in a week.

"I didn't see any lights on. I'm guessing they've gone to visit Martha's mother. They always do it on Christmas Eve, no matter what. Despite the circumstances, I'm sure they'd keep up with tradition."

Hannah stayed out of the house, holding the reins to the buggy tightly in her hands. This was to be the final delivery. Afterward, she would return home to her siblings with her husband.

Earlier that year, she and Noah had married. Over the 18 months before the wedding, he had blossomed, coming out of his shell completely. He attended every community event he could, never missed a church service, and became a steady presence in her life.

When they married, he sold his house and moved in with his new wife and her siblings. They welcomed Noah into the family with open arms, seeing how happy he made their older sister.

Hannah's only regret was that her parents weren't there to see the wedding. But she knew they were watching over her, and maybe they had even sent Noah into her life to bless her with happiness.

Now, she no longer had to worry about finances or security. She, and by extension her siblings, were well-provided for. She could focus on giving them the best life possible.

Leah, who was now 17, had started attending Sunday singings just last month. Before long, she too would begin courting. It was an exciting time for everyone.

Noah had continued his tradition of playing Secret Santa, and now he had his new wife involved. They kept the secret from the rest of the family. Hannah suspected that Leah knew, but if so, she was sensible enough to keep it to herself. But they never discussed it, and because of Hannah's promise to Noah two years ago, they never would.

"*Kumm* on, let's go," Noah said, watching the Miller farmhouse carefully.

Hannah made a clicking noise with her tongue, and the horse moved forward.

She pulled up in front of the Miller house, and Noah jumped off the buggy without hesitation.

"Give me a hand with this one, it's a bit heavy," he said, looking up at his wife.

Hannah hesitated. "You'll be okay. You're strong."

She watched guiltily as he grunted and struggled with the parcel. "It'd be easier if you helped."

"*Kumm* on, hurry up," Hannah said, glancing down the drive. "They could be here any moment."

Finally, Noah got the gift in place. He set the card with his beautiful calligraphy on top. Noah had explained to Hannah how his mother had taught him to write so gracefully. Watching him expertly craft each card for the gifts was one of her great joys.

He returned to the buggy, out of breath.

"Well done," she said and guided the horse down the driveway. Fortunately, there had been no snow over Christmas this year, so no tracks would betray their visit. When the Millers returned, the gift would be waiting for them.

"Don't worry, I'll make sure you're well-fed when we get home," Hannah said, glancing at her panting husband beside her.

"It would've been a little easier if you had helped," he objected.

Hannah hesitated, then brought the buggy to a halt. "*Jah*, I know, but..." she paused, searching for the right words.

Noah looked confused. "What?"

"Let's just say it's not recommended that I lift anything heavy..." she stopped speaking again and then added softly, "in my condition."

"Have you pulled your back or something?" Noah asked, still puzzled. Suddenly, realization dawned on him. He looked into his wife's eyes, and he knew. "Are we...are we having a *boppli*?"

Hannah nodded. "*Jah*. I'm pregnant."

Noah couldn't help himself; he flung his arms around his wife and held her close.

"I love Christmas," he murmured. "It's the most magical time of the year."

STAY IN TOUCH

Join my super fans and become the very first to hear about new releases, special offers and free books. Sign up below.

CLICK HERE TO BE THE FIRST TO KNOW

Rebecca's Redemption

Rebecca sacrificed her happiness to save her family, losing the love of her life, David, in the process. After her husband Amos dies, Rebecca uncovers his hidden secrets and faces an unexpected second chance with David. As they unite to save their community from rising floodwaters, Rebecca's journey reveals the strength of love, sacrifice, and hope for a new beginning.

A Second Chance for the Bishop's Heart

A decade after their love was shattered by a single moment, Hannah and Samuel are thrust back into each other's lives when a sudden loss brings her back to their Amish community. Now the community's bishop, Samuel, sees a chance to correct past mistakes, but faces opposition from a man who will try to keep them apart. As Hannah stands at a crossroads, she must decide whether to rekindle their long-lost love or avoid the inevitable turmoil her return will cause.

The Amish Wedding Match

After ending a brief courtship, Naomi's mother insists on matchmaking her with the handsome Amish farmer, Leroy. A dangerous incident and an unlikely rescuer force Naomi to choose between her mother's wishes and following her heart. As her best friend's wedding nears, Naomi devises a plan to find true love, realizing the path is far from easy.

Amish Echoes

When Jonas courts Sarah, his brother Aaron silently harbors his own feelings for her. Tragedy strikes when Jonas dies in an accident, leaving Aaron consumed by guilt and isolating himself, despite the growing bond with Sarah. Guided by the Bishop's words and faced with a life-changing decision, Aaron must choose between surrendering to his grief or embracing the chance for love and happiness in their Amish community.

Love's Shadow

Ruth's childhood memories of the Weaver brothers, Daniel and Amos, evolve into a love triangle as she grows older, drawn to Daniel's charm despite his rebellious ways. As Amos diligently works to maintain the family farm and secretly loves Ruth, he feels overshadowed by his brother. When Daniel's rejection of their Amish lifestyle forces Ruth to make a life-altering decision, she must choose between fleeting charm and true love, guided by her faith.

The Beekeeper

Anna isn't interested in courting, much to her mother's dismay, until she's reluctantly charmed by the handsome Moses. Meanwhile, Anna's unexpected connection with the quiet beekeeper Stephen deepens, even as she tries to honor her courtship with Moses. As Anna navigates her feelings, a secret threatens to change everything, making her question whether Moses or Stephen holds the key to her happily ever after.

Seeking Naomi's Heart

Naomi's parents are eager to see her court Elmer, unaware of her secret love for her Englischer boss, Marcus. Despite her best friend's warnings, Naomi's infatuation with Marcus deepens, straining her friendships and leading her to a crossroads. Confronted with life-changing events, Naomi must decide whether to follow her heart or heed the advice of those who care for her, determining who will ultimately claim her heart.

DOWNLOAD NOW

Made in the USA
Middletown, DE
05 November 2024